Happy 2[...] [...]

May the next 25 years be as much fun!

Love, as always,

Carole Mortimer

Dear Reader,

What a pleasure and privilege it is to be part of Harlequin Presents®' twenty-fifth birthday celebration. For twenty-one of those years I have been a Harlequin author, and my fiftieth book is due in North America later this year. I hope that Harlequin and I will still be around for a long time yet, giving pleasure to millions of women around the world. Please write and tell me if you enjoy *Lovers' Lies,* and ask for a newsletter so you won't miss my next Harlequin Presents®. Box 18240, Glen Innes, Auckland, New Zealand.

Daphne

Daphne Clair

DAPHNE CLAIR

Lovers' Lies

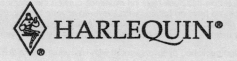

HARLEQUIN®

TORONTO • NEW YORK • LONDON
AMSTERDAM • PARIS • SYDNEY • HAMBURG
STOCKHOLM • ATHENS • TOKYO • MILAN • MADRID
PRAGUE • WARSAW • BUDAPEST • AUCKLAND

ISBN 0-373-11970-4

LOVERS' LIES

First North American Publication 1998.

Copyright © 1997 by Daphne Clair.

This edition published by arrangement with Harlequin Books S.A.

® and TM are trademarks of the publisher. Trademarks indicated with ® are registered in the United States Patent and Trademark Office, the Canadian Trade Marks Office and in other countries.

Printed in U.S.A.

CHAPTER ONE

BEIJING was the last place Felicia expected to meet Joshua Tagget again.

She had landed in China the night before, jet-lagged and in dire need of sleep following the eighteen-hour journey from New Zealand. After breakfasting in her room and coming down to the hotel lobby to meet her tour guide and the other members of her party, she still felt glassy-eyed and woolly-headed.

When her gaze lit on the well-remembered dark amber eyes under black brows, she was sure she must be hallucinating. The dreams in which Joshua Tagget used to feature had stopped, thank heaven, a few years after the events that had shattered her childhood.

His brows twitched upward in interrogation, and it dawned on her that he was dismayingly real, and also that her instant recognition wasn't mutual. She was twenty-five years old and any resemblance to the impressionable, romantic thirteen-year-old he had briefly known had long since vanished.

Joshua had been the epitome of her ideal man, the fantasy figure that had woken her first immature stirrings of sexuality, and as unattainable to her as any pop star or film idol. Thank heaven she'd at least had the sense to hide her palpitating interest in him, hugging it to her like a delicious secret until her fragile feelings were cruelly shattered in heartbreak and disillusion.

5

He had barely altered; perhaps his shoulders were a shade broader, but otherwise he looked as lithe and lean as a panther. A small crease in his cheek emphasised the slight, enquiring lift at one corner of a chiselled mouth, and the tiny fanned lines by his eyes added an attractive maturity to his classic good looks. Even so, he appeared considerably younger than... She calculated rapidly that he must be thirty-seven or thereabouts.

'Miss Felicia Stevens?' the guide said, looking round the loose group of two dozen or so.

'Yes.' Felicia stepped forward. Now Joshua would surely recognise her. She could still feel his gaze—alert, amused, intrigued. Putting a totally wrong interpretation on her shocked stare.

The guide was a slim Chinese woman with smooth, pretty features and glossy bobbed hair, who invited the tour party to call her Jen or Jenny. She gave Felicia a dazzling smile and handed her a name tag, encased in plastic, and a linen carry-bag identical to those most of the group now held, before consulting her list again. 'Mr Jo-sua Tagget?'

'Here.' Joshua took the plastic label and the bag the woman held out to him, his gaze sliding reluctantly away from Felicia. One of the other women spoke to him, and he bent his head slightly to listen, then threw it back in laughter.

Felicia heard the blood pounding in her head, felt the need to take an extra deep breath. He didn't know her. Only two feet away from her, he hadn't recognised her at all. Even her name had rung no bell of memory.

She ought to have been relieved, but her chief emotion was overwhelming anger. It was as if he had wiped all recollection of that hideous summer from his mind. Something she could never do. Never in a million years.

Shaking, she clutched the bag in her hand, her fingers clenching tightly on the limp straps. A middle-aged, dumpy woman standing nearby said in an unmistakably American accent, 'Are you OK, honey?'

She must look pale. Mustering a smile, Felicia said, 'Yes, thank you. It's a bit hot.'

'Oh, yeah,' the woman agreed. 'I hope the bus is air-conditioned.'

Jen was gathering her charges, hurrying them towards the door where a blue and white bus had pulled up a few minutes ago. 'Miss Stevens?' She had noticed that Felicia wasn't moving along with the others. 'Come,' she said, flapping a hand with quick, anxious little movements, 'please?'

Felicia hesitated. She could say she was unwell, that she couldn't make the trip today after all. Then she'd contact her travel agent, see if she could transfer to another tour...

'Miss Stevens?' The guide was looking puzzled. 'You have forgotten something?'

No, she wanted to say. I've forgotten nothing. If only I could... Joshua Tagget seems to have successfully forgotten. He didn't even blink an eyelid when you said my name.

She'd prepaid in New Zealand for this tour. Three weeks, all expenses included. It had cost her a lot of money and, realistically, she didn't suppose there'd be any chance of changing the arrangements at this late hour. The tour company wouldn't look kindly on a request for a refund. 'No,' she said. 'It's all right.' She walked forward as if moving through water, and followed the guide outside.

The bus was filling up. Joshua had got himself a window seat. That didn't surprise Felicia. Nor was she surprised that the best-looking woman in the party, a fresh-faced brunette with long hair waving to her shoulders and green eyes accentuated by thickly applied mascara and eyeliner, sat beside him. Joshua was looking out the window while the woman settled herself, tucking her bag under the seat. Passing them, Felicia wondered if they were together, or if the woman was just hopeful.

A group of young women occupied the rear bench seat, three fit-looking young men nearby eyeing them with covert interest. Middle-aged couples, a family with two children, and a few apparently unattached singles of both sexes made up the rest of the tour party. The small American woman, with a seat to herself, beckoned Felicia. 'You can sit here if you like. I'm all alone.'

'Thank you.' Me too, Felicia thought. It had been that way for years, and usually she didn't mind. Perhaps it was being in a strange country, among strangers, that caused a sudden wave of melancholy.

'I'm Maggie,' the American woman said. 'Maggie Price. And you're Felicia. Such a pretty name. It suits you.'

'Thank you.' Felicia smiled, brushing back from her cheek an ear-level strand of hair the colour of dark manuka honey.

The door closed smoothly with an airy sigh as the driver pulled out from the hotel and veered around one of dozens of yellow taxis weaving through the bicycles thronging the broad road.

'I hope we can go shopping here later,' Maggie remarked as they roared past market stalls set out under spreading shade trees on the pavements.

At a street corner a group of elderly men squatted around a card game. The woman sitting beside Joshua Tagget stood up, put a camera to her eye, and leaned across him to take a picture of them. Her colourful low-necked sunfrock must have allowed him an enjoyable view of a fairly spectacular cleavage.

Cat, Felicia scolded herself. She'd long since given up wishing for a more generous endowment in that department, or for shiny black hair and sea-green eyes, a smaller nose and larger hips.

She didn't regret having had her over-prominent teeth straightened, even though it had meant two years with a mouthful of metal, and by now she knew that the long legs that had made her gawky and self-consciously taller than her classmates at twelve were an asset rather than a liability. The figure she'd finally developed as a late-blooming teenager was adequate if not sensational, the envy of many of her friends who constantly battled with their weight.

She'd dyed her hair once and it made her look like something out of *The Munsters*. These days she contented herself with an occasional strawberry rinse to give it extra life in winter. Some people professed to find her emphatically blue eyes beautiful, and she used eye-shadow sparingly to intensify their colour, as well as mascara to darken and lengthen her lashes.

The engine throbbed warningly and Joshua's seat companion sat down again as they shot off round the corner, the driver blasting his horn with little visible effect on the massed cyclists.

Maggie put a hand to her chest and inhaled sharply as the bus narrowly missed an oblivious rider pulling a cart piled high with woven baskets. But she soon recovered.

'Oh, look!' she said, pointing. A teenage girl in a bright red regional costume stood hawking embroidered goods outside a building that combined twentieth-century business architecture with the distinctive curved roof lines of the Orient.

Felicia was grateful for the novelty of the passing scene, and the need to respond to Maggie's excited comments. She couldn't push Joshua Tagget entirely out of her mind, but at least he could be relegated to the fringes.

Eventually they drew up outside the looming pink wall of the Forbidden City. Emerging into blinding sun, Felicia put on dark glasses and the wide-brimmed hat she'd been advised to bring. She'd used sunscreen before leaving the hotel, and dropped the tube into her bag. She hoped the brunette now standing alongside Joshua while the guide waited for the rest of the party to alight had done the same. The woman had very fair skin, contrasting with Joshua's tan. They made a striking couple.

Pain twisted inside Felicia, translating into anger as fierce as it was illogical. She could hardly expect the man to spend the rest of his life mourning the events of twelve years ago. But, she thought bitterly, watching the sunlight catch the surprising russet lights in the darkness of his hair as he bent his head and smiled at the woman beside him, he needn't look so damned untouched, so impervious.

As if he'd felt the intensity of her gaze, he turned his head in her direction, and she hastily looked away, fol-

lowing the guide through the Tiananmen Gate, opposite
the vast, famous square.

In the enormous cobbled courtyards, black-clad gar-
deners were painstakingly removing weeds and grass in
the continuing work of restoration. As the tour party
crossed the baking hot stones Felicia mentally clothed
the crowds of Chinese sightseers in the sumptuous,
graceful fashion of the courtiers and servants who had
once lived and worked here.

Leaning on the barrier at the doorway of The Palace
of Heavenly Purity to photograph a wonderful dragon
screen behind the high throne, she found herself standing
next to Joshua Tagget, his arm brushing briefly against
hers.

Felicia stepped hastily back, and he turned his head.
'Sorry,' he murmured. His eyes lingered on her—not too
blatantly, but in the manner of a man appreciating a
good-looking woman, and with a hint of interested
enquiry.

Felicia managed a tight smile before she walked away,
ostensibly to photograph one of the bronze cranes on
the terrace, and heard Joshua's deep voice ask Jen a
question about the intricate carved ceiling of the throne
room. She felt her hands clench, and with a sense of
rising panic wondered how she was going to stand three
weeks of his proximity.

There was some comfort at least in knowing he had
no idea who she was. She would just keep out of his
way as much as possible and pretend they had never met.
There was no reason to let his presence destroy her
enjoyment.

By the time the party had passed through the Gate of
Earthly Tranquillity to the Imperial Garden where plants

and trees gave an illusion of coolness, they were relieved to take a rest.

The guide pointed out two intertwined old trees. 'They are called "the love trees".'

Joshua laughed quietly, and Felicia thought with unaccustomed viciousness, Yes, you can laugh at love—it was always a game to you.

But it hadn't been a game to poor Genevieve. Genevieve had died for it, while Joshua walked away unscathed.

They left the Forbidden City for the Summer Palace and lunch at the Ting Li Guan restaurant. 'This means in English, the Pavilion for Listening to the Orioles Sing,' Jen informed them.

'Oh, isn't that charming!' Maggie exclaimed.

'Lovely,' Felicia agreed, manoeuvring herself into a chair as far from Joshua Tagget as possible before taking off her hat and sunglasses. She was surprised to find that she was hungry as well as thirsty. Tucking into prawns, rice and something deep-fried that was unfamiliar but delicious, she almost managed to forget the man she'd been carefully avoiding all morning.

The restaurant lay on a lake shore, and after eating they were taken across the water in a canopied boat with a dragon's head at the bow. Seated at one side of the boat between Maggie and a young couple holding hands, Felicia removed her sunglasses to focus her camera on a series of glittering curved roofs gracing the steep, wooded hillside above the lake. She felt a breeze tug at her hat, and was too late to save it from being whisked off her head.

It didn't fly straight to the water, but instead skimmed a few yards along the boat, where a tanned, masculine hand stretched out and captured it.

A few people laughed and applauded, and Felicia stood up—just as Joshua did the same, her hat still held in his hand.

He stepped towards her and, her hair whipping about her face, she reached for the hat. 'Thank you.'

'My pleasure.' He was smiling, but with a faint frown between his brows as if he was trying to place her. His gaze dropped momentarily to her name tag. 'I'd hang onto the headgear if I were you.'

'Yes,' she said, and returned to her seat.

Instead of reclaiming his own he followed her, placing a hand on one of the posts supporting the canopy above them as he looked down at her.

Felicia turned her face away, studying the hired canoes and other small ferries dotting the ruffled waters of the lake.

'I know it's an old line,' Joshua said, 'but do I know you from somewhere?'

Felicia swallowed before turning an indifferent, clear blue gaze on him. 'You're right,' she said coolly, not bothering to lower her voice, then paused. 'It is an old line.'

She turned again to contemplate the view. Maggie made a small, protesting sound. The male half of the young couple cast Joshua a sympathetic glance, and the girl smothered a giggle.

Felicia couldn't see the expression on Joshua's face as he received the very public snub, but after a moment she heard him laugh softly, and then he removed his hand from the post and strolled away.

A few seconds later Maggie said tentatively, 'He seems quite a nice young man.'

'I'm sure he is,' Felicia agreed, lying in her teeth. Joshua Taggett was far from being nice, and she had cause to know it. She withdrew her aching eyes from the view and smiled at the American woman.

'Do you have someone back home?' Maggie asked curiously.

Felicia shook her head. 'No. I'm just not interested.'

'Oh.' Maggie looked over at Joshua, standing with his back to them now near the bow. 'Well, let me tell you, I think you're picky. If I were ten years younger...maybe make that fifteen...'

Felicia laughed, and saw Joshua quickly turn his head, his eyes homing in on her. He probably thought they were laughing at him. Well, let him think it. She dragged her gaze away.

After peeking at some of the jade and ivory treasures in the buildings near the foreshore, Maggie and most of the older members of the party elected to stroll along the broad winding paths seeking both beauty and shade, while others climbed the steep flights of steps to the Pavilion of Precious Clouds.

The pavilion seemed to have grown from the uneven grey rocks, they were so perfectly blended. Children scrambled happily about among the rocks and the several flights of stairs, watched fondly by their parents. In the gatehouse a small girl in a white frilly dress, white socks and shiny patent leather shoes gazed with awe at two huge ceramic statues with beetling eyebrows and fearsome snarls.

As Felicia stopped beside her the little girl regarded her with as much interest as she had the guardians of the gateway, and said carefully, 'Hello.'

'Hello,' Felicia returned, 'little princess.'

The child's parents arrived, panting with exertion. The father picked his daughter up, smoothing her black hair away from her eyes. As Felicia made to turn away the man with signs and smiles urged her to pose with his wife and daughter while he took a picture. Felicia obliged, and then the family posed for her.

She began to make her way down again to the lakeside, only to dodge back into the shadow of the gatehouse as she caught sight of Joshua Tagget ascending the steps.

She hurried back through the gateway and took the nearest flight of steps, arriving in a small square tower. Miraculously, the narrow room was empty. An arched opening down to floor level framed a view across tiled rooftops to the vast plain below. Just beyond the opening a low stone wall hardly impeded the eye. Felicia raised her camera for the obligatory picture.

Moving to just inside the archway, she stooped for a shot of an intriguing orange-tiled roof angle, and as she straightened and turned to the doorway the space was filled by the shadowy figure of a man.

Joshua. Instinctively she stepped backwards, forgetting the open archway. Her feet struck the low barrier and she gasped and threw out a hand towards the wall, her heart plunging in fright.

With a sharp exclamation Joshua lunged forward and grabbed her arm, dragging her towards him so that she came up hard against his chest.

She inhaled the smell of soap and fresh sweat, and her cheek was momentarily pressed against his cotton shirt, warm from the sun and his body.

Then his hands were on both her arms, holding her away from him. And his voice, harsh with shock, demanded, 'What the hell is the matter with you?'

'You startled me,' Felicia said. 'I...didn't hear anyone come in.'

His hands dropped. 'Sorry.' But his clipped voice told her he thought she was a fool. 'I wasn't following you. The message on the boat was loud and clear.'

And he wouldn't bother pursuing a woman who had made her lack of interest plain. Felicia wondered where the buxom brunette had got to. 'Thank you,' she said stiffly. 'Although I wasn't really likely to fall. I just got a fright.'

A Chinese family appeared in the doorway and politely hung back.

'It's OK, I'm leaving,' Felicia said, gesturing them to come in as she slipped through the opening.

Joshua pointedly remained standing at the top of the steps as she descended them. She could feel his eyes boring into her back until she made the shelter of the dim, shaded gateway.

Some meals were included in the tour, but Jen recommended several Beijing restaurants for those who wanted to try them. Maggie suggested she and Felicia have a drink in the hotel bar on their return from the Summer Palace and plan their evening.

Others had the same idea. The three young men had joined the party of young women in one corner of the crowded bar, and two middle-aged couples from the tour group called to Maggie and Felicia to join them.

One couple was Australian, the other American, and in the course of the day they had already established a rapport. After enquiring which part of the world she came from, the American man said, 'There's another New Zealander on the tour. Joshua—you know him?'

'We met this morning.'

A waitress came to take their orders. Her English was earnest but limited, and there was much laughter and international sign language.

While Felicia was talking to the Australian couple the American man hailed someone coming in and began pulling up more chairs. It wasn't until the newcomers sat down that Felicia turned, the smile freezing on her face when she saw who had joined them. Joshua, with the brunette beauty—now wearing loose, cool white trousers and a red figure-hugging top—back at his side.

His mouth turned down at one corner as he acknowledged her presence, his eyes holding a wry amusement. He knew she didn't want to be anywhere near him, and thought it was funny.

Introductions were made all round, and Felicia smiled nicely at the dark-haired girl whose name was given as Suzette. Perfect for her, Felicia thought, and looked away to watch the waitress fill a tray at the bar.

She drank the mineral water she had ordered, taking no part in the plans for dinner at an outside restaurant. They all seemed happy to stick together, and she decided that if Joshua was going to join them she was bowing out.

Felicia had emptied her glass and was formulating the words to leave when someone ordered another round of drinks, and she found a second glass placed before her.

But when there was a general move to leave she said quietly to Maggie, 'I'd really rather have a snack and go to bed. I haven't recovered from the flight. Enjoy your evening.' At least Maggie wouldn't lack for company.

The other woman looked disappointed but didn't argue. 'Well ... see you in the morning, then.'

Unlike Suzette, Felicia hadn't been to her room to change. Thinking she would freshen up before having a light meal, she made for the elevators.

Two arrived at the same time, and she let the other people who were waiting fill the first, stepping into the second. The doors were already closing after her when a strong male hand made them re-open and Joshua entered.

She thought he almost stepped out again, but changed his mind, allowing the doors to slide to and shut them in.

Startled, Felicia said, 'Aren't you going to dinner?'

He turned to lean on the wall beside him as the car started upwards. 'Not with that crowd.' After a short pause, he added, 'I thought *you* were going with them.'

'They're all very nice people.'

His eyebrows twitched. 'Sure. So why *aren't* you with them?'

She could say that she'd been trying to avoid him. But studied rudeness wasn't natural to her and besides, if she made an issue of this he'd begin to wonder why. 'My plane was delayed for twelve hours at Auckland,' she

said, 'and my connection in Hong Kong had to be re-
scheduled. I need an early night.'

The elevator slid to a halt and the doors opened, but
the two people waiting gestured that they wanted to go
down, not up.

As the doors closed again Joshua said, 'I really did
wonder if we'd met somewhere. The way you looked at
me in the lobby this morning...perhaps I
misinterpreted?'

'You remind me of someone I used to know,' Felicia
prevaricated. 'That's all.'

He nodded, his eyes uncomfortably alert and as-
sessing. If he asked who, she was going to have to chance
a direct lie. But when he spoke he said mildly, 'If I'd
been trying to pick you up I'd have thought of something slightly more original. Like—if you're going to eat
before this early night you say you need, would you care
to join me?' His mouth curved invitingly, and his in-
quiring eyes gleamed with humour.

'That's original?' Felicia asked dryly before she could
stop herself.

He laughed. 'At least it's less hackneyed than "Haven't
we met before?" The Bamboo Grove on the ground floor
serves a buffet of mixed western and Chinese food. I
thought I'd try it tonight.'

The elevator halted at her floor, and as the doors glided
apart he said, 'So, may I meet you there?'

'I'm really not very hungry.' She stepped out into the
corridor.

He held the door. 'If you change your mind I'll be
there at seven-thirty.'

By the time she turned to tell him she wouldn't be,
the doors were closing again.

CHAPTER TWO

FELICIA showered in lukewarm water to cool herself, then dressed in fresh undies and a loose, short-skirted dress. Her excuse of being in more need of sleep than food hadn't been entirely specious, but by the time she'd unpacked a few things that she hadn't had time earlier to take from her suitcase, and studied the material provided about the hotel services and the city of Beijing, she was surprised to find herself feeling both wide awake and hungry.

She could order from room service.

Menu in hand, she glanced out the window at the tree-lined street, still full of bicycles and people. An old couple wearing woven peasant hats and comfortable pyjama-like garments exchanged greetings with a group of young women in colourful cotton dresses. Rickshaw cyclists cruised by, their vehicles sporting fringed canopies and cushioned interiors.

She was in an exciting, mysterious, ancient country—and here she was contemplating spending the evening sitting in her hotel room because she was reluctant to face a man who had disappeared from her life when she was no more than a child.

Ridiculous, she said to herself. She'd have a quick meal downstairs and venture forth for a little exploration on her own.

It wasn't until she was approaching the restaurant that she looked at her watch and saw with surprise that the time was just after seven-thirty.

'Miss Stevens?' A smiling waiter greeted her at the door, his dark eyes gleaming.

'Yes,' she said hesitantly. Service at the hotel was excellent, but surely the staff couldn't memorise all the guests' names?

'This way.' He beamed at her and led her round the tall circular buffet topped with its own porcelain-tiled roof, and ushered her to a table for two. Joshua rose from his seat as the waiter pulled out a chair for her.

'Glad you changed your mind,' Joshua said.

Felicia had stopped dead. The waiter looked at her expectantly. She cast a glance around, saw the dining room appeared to be full, and reluctantly sank into the seat.

'I will bring a wine list now,' the waiter promised in faultless English, and bustled gracefully away as Joshua resumed his seat.

'I thought I'd better grab a table,' Joshua explained.

Felicia sat stiffly. 'You told the waiter you were expecting me?'

'I tipped him well to watch out for you.'

'I thought tipping wasn't acceptable here.'

'In hotels that deal with western tourists it's probably not uncommon.'

'I appreciate your keeping a seat for me,' she said, 'but . . . if you don't mind I'll ask for a separate check.'

Joshua regarded her thoughtfully. 'And if I do mind?' he enquired. 'After all, I did invite you to eat with me.'

'I prefer to pay my own way.'

He shrugged. 'If you insist. Is it necessary to tell you that I don't think buying you a meal will entitle me to any privileges?'

'It isn't necessary at all,' Felicia assured him coolly, 'since you're not buying it.'

'Hmm.' He leaned back in his chair, his eyes speculative as they rested on her. The waiter brought the wine list and Joshua took it and murmured thanks without shifting his gaze from Felicia. 'I hope you'll share a bottle of wine with me, all the same,' he said. 'My treat. Or do you only drink mineral water?'

She was surprised he'd noticed what she was drinking earlier. She'd thought Suzette had been claiming most of his attention. 'I drink wine,' she said, 'sometimes.' This afternoon she'd felt slightly dehydrated and cool water was the most sensible thing to drink. But a glass of wine with her meal was a decidedly pleasant prospect. The fact that Joshua's very presence across the table was causing her skin to prickle with antagonism was beside the point.

'What would you like? White or red?'

'White—if that's OK with you.'

He flashed her a smile. 'Fine. Medium or dry?'

'Usually I prefer dry, but I'd like to sample something local.'

'Good. We have something in common after all. Now, let's see . . .'

He drew her into the choosing process, making it a discussion, and they settled on a bottle of Huadong Chardonnay. When the waiter offered a menu both opted for the buffet. 'Miss Stevens would like a separate check,' Joshua added without a blink.

The buffet was laden with such a variety that Felicia found herself eating more than she had meant to, supplementing delicious Chinese dishes with a small bowl of fluffy white rice and a crisp salad.

And of course it was impossible not to talk. Joshua asked where she lived, what she did. 'Auckland,' she said. 'I'm a partner in a boutique-style shop specialising in bedroom and bathroom furnishings and accessories.'

She kept her voice crisp and emotionless, with no hint of defensiveness. Some men made suggestive remarks when she told them what her business was about, but Joshua just nodded interestedly and asked questions about her target market, type of stock, and supplier base.

'I've been to a trade fair here,' he said, 'hoping to open doors for the agricultural machinery my company makes. We've been using a middleman in Hong Kong, but I wanted to see something of the country for myself and follow up a few contacts.'

'Your company? You own it?' She tried to keep the surprise from her voice, make it a casual query.

'That's right.'

She schooled her face to indifference and bit her tongue on the questions hovering at its tip—how, since when, where had a young handyman with a lawn-mowing round acquired an international business? She said, 'There are special tours for business groups.'

'None of them were quite what I wanted, and this one seems a good introduction to the country. Being an independent traveller can be pretty frustrating when you don't know the language and have limited time.'

They talked for a while of what they'd seen that day, and swapped random knowledge of Chinese history and culture.

'I've read a couple of books,' Joshua said, 'but the more I learn, the more I know there is to learn.'

Felicia smiled, surprising herself. The food and wine must have had a mellowing effect. 'It's a huge country, with a long, long history. I started reading about it months ago, but it would take a lifetime to learn it all.'

A flare of warmth and masculine interest in his eyes as he returned the smile told her that he wasn't unaware of her as a female. From Joshua Tagget she found that faintly shocking, and had to remind herself that not only was she a grown woman now, he had no idea who she was, no memory of the teenage girl he had once known. But it was startling to find her cheeks heating slightly under the veiled curiosity in his gaze, and a disturbing sexual reaction to him tingling along her veins.

They skipped dessert, and Felicia declined coffee, instead asking for her bill.

'And mine,' Joshua said. As the waiter went to get them he turned to Felicia. 'Do you have plans for the rest of the evening?'

'I . . . was thinking of walking a bit before I turn in.'

'I wouldn't mind walking off that meal. A lone woman shouldn't wander round on her own at night,' Joshua said.

'I believe China is pretty safe, actually.'

'Maybe, but you'd be even safer with me.'

Something must have quivered in her expression. He queried, 'You don't believe that?'

'You think I should take your word for it?'

He turned up his palms in a gesture of defeat. 'You want references?'

'Do you have any on you?'

Joshua grinned. 'As a matter of fact I have a couple of quite impressive letters of introduction—they came in useful at the trade fair—but I've left them in my room.'

The waiter brought the bills and laid them on the table. Felicia signed her name and room number and picked up her bag.

As she stood up, Joshua followed. 'So,' he said, 'do I have to go and fetch my references?'

'Of course not.'

Felicia was pretty sure that if she went off by herself he would follow her anyway. Discreetly, perhaps at a distance, but—ironically—he was the sort of man who couldn't knowingly let a woman walk alone down dark streets in a strange city.

The air was warm and heavy. The shops and street stalls had closed up but there were still people sitting on low stools outside their homes, playing cards or chess. Passing under an overhanging tree that cast a deep shadow on the pavement, Felicia stumbled a little on an uneven flagstone and Joshua took her arm to steady her.

'OK?' he said.

'Yes.' She pulled away slightly and he released his hold. Felicia hoped he hadn't discerned the small shiver that his brief grip on her arm had evoked.

A black-clad elderly woman approached accompanied by a boy of about twelve years old, already taller than she was. 'Hello,' the young boy said. 'How are you?' The old woman smiled proudly as Felicia and Joshua returned the greeting. Cooking smells wafted onto the street from a rattling air-conditioning unit set in a nearby wall. The city had a hot, heavy, alien aroma.

The weight of centuries and the burden of a teeming population seemed to scent the very air.

They skirted a high corrugated iron fence with silent cranes inside it towering against the fading sky. The pavement was strewn with heaps of dirt and broken bits of wood and plaster.

'Rebuilding,' Joshua said, pausing briefly to peer through a peephole in the fence. 'Whatever it is, it's going to be big.' He straightened and came back to her side.

'I wonder how the others are enjoying their dinner,' she said, making a random effort at conversation to divert her own attention from her stupid sensitivity to his nearness.

'Sorry you didn't join them?' he asked.

'No, of course not.' Her denial was probably too quick, too emphatic. 'The hotel food is very good—don't you agree?'

'Very,' he assented gravely. Obviously he didn't think much of her conversational powers. He wasn't alone in that. Apart from anything else, now that she was sure he had no notion who she was it seemed simplest to keep things that way. She had no desire to discuss the past with Joshua Tagget, and ruin her holiday.

They reached the corner and Joshua said, 'Round the block?'

'Yes, OK.'

They walked in silence for a while. Felicia wondered if Joshua was wishing he'd joined the others. Suzette would miss him. 'I'm not very good company,' she said, despising herself for making excuses to him. But the silence had become too fraught for her, loaded with old memories and the new, unsettling reactions she was experiencing, too strong to ignore but too contradictory and perilous to make sense of.

'Why do you say that?'

'I'm too... tired to make conversation.'

'If I'd wanted conversation I'd have gone to dinner with the crowd. I've had a very pleasant evening.'

They came to another corner and Felicia blindly changed direction, heading—she hoped—towards the hotel. Simple courtesy demanded that she say she had also enjoyed the evening. But for her it had been too emotionally charged.

She quickened her pace, and suddenly the road disappeared into an unlit alleyway. She stopped abruptly, and felt Joshua's presence at her back, not quite touching her. 'We've taken a wrong turning,' she said.

'Maybe.'

'We'll have to go back to the main road.'

As she made to retrace their steps, he stopped her with a hand on her arm. 'But there's light through there, and another road, see?'

She peered into the dimness, and saw at the end of the alley people passing back and forth, and a road with traffic, bicycles.

'Never go back,' Joshua suggested, 'unless there's no other way out.'

Felicia shrugged. There was something to be said, she grudgingly supposed, for having a male companion. Sensible women automatically avoided lonely, dark streets. She let him lead her forward.

One side of the alley was lined with dozens of bicycles standing silent and gleaming side by side in the gloom. On the other side were closed back doors.

Then quite quickly the alleyway emerged into a broad street, and she recognised that they were close to the hotel.

When they re-entered the lobby a few minutes later it seemed very bright and spacious.

'A nightcap?' Joshua suggested. 'The bar's still open.'

'Not for me,' Felicia decided. 'Thank you for your company.' She had to get away from him to sort out the confusion of her feelings.

Joshua ignored the hand she held out. 'I don't want to drink alone. I'll be going up to bed too. Tomorrow it's the Great Wall, isn't it? Stamina may be required.'

There weren't many people about and they had the elevator to themselves. When the doors slid open at Felicia's floor, Joshua surprised her by taking her shoulders and turning her gently but firmly to face him.

She hardly had time to register the taut, questioning look on his face, the deep light in his tigerish eyes, before he bent his head and pressed a warm, insistent, exploratory kiss against her mouth.

Taken unawares, she felt her lips quiver and part under his before she could stop herself.

Then she was free, and he had raised a hand to hold the door for her. She stepped back, staring at him, and heard him say, 'Goodnight, Felicia,' before the doors closed and she was left blinking at the bright red arrow above her.

'...the only man-made structure visible from outer space.'

Felicia stood on the Great Wall, only half listening to the rapid-fire statistics Jen was giving the group huddled around her. 'Two thousand, one hundred and fifty miles long . . . three hundred thousand workers . . .'

Hundreds of tourists of various nationalities milled about, climbing the worn steps and squinting at the farther reaches of the wall where a shifting tide of people thinned as it receded into the distance.

A hand on the hard stone parapet, Felicia gazed at the desolate, rock-strewn countryside. She'd read the figures, but none of them had prepared her for the feeling of actually being here—for the sense of the toiling of time, of generations that had lived and died and loved and been forgotten since the building of the wall had begun.

'And this is only a remnant,' Joshua's voice said beside her. 'Pretty impressive, isn't it?'

'Awesome,' Felicia agreed. She had to force herself to look at him, the sound of his voice bringing back a vivid memory of that brief, unexpected kiss last night.

Not quite meeting his eyes, she gave him a quick smile and moved to merge into the group following Jen along the top of the wall.

She had the feeling that he remained staring after her for a few seconds before he joined them, but by that time she was walking with Maggie, successfully ignoring him.

Suzette unwittingly assisted her to do so for the rest of the day, attaching herself to Joshua's side and making sure that whatever attention he could spare from sightseeing was directed to her. Felicia ought to have been grateful. Instead she found herself harbouring uncharitable thoughts about both of them—Suzette for her blatant man-chasing, and Joshua because of his air of amused tolerance. Patronising, she labelled it caustically.

It occurred to her that she was being a dog in the manger, and the thought only made her more irritated. Her muddled feelings were a hangover, she had decided last night, gazing into the sleepless darkness of her room, residual emotion from her early adolescence, when she'd thought Joshua was the handsomest, most romantic man on earth.

Face it, she told herself brutally as she changed for dinner back at the hotel after their return from the Great Wall. He was your first crush, your puppy-love, and despite everything that happened, somewhere deep down traces of those feelings are still buried in your subconscious.

That was why she had found his casual kiss last night so disturbing. At thirteen she'd at least had enough sense to know that a grown man like Joshua Tagget wasn't going to be interested in a barely pubescent girl. She had been happy to abet his love affair with Genevieve—a form of transference, she now supposed.

Had he ever divined her own feelings—that excruciating blend of half-understood, heavily romanticised sexual awakening and blind hero-worship? God, she hoped not! She grew hot at the thought, suddenly reverting to uncomfortable adolescent self-consciousness.

Tonight everyone was dining in the hotel because they were scheduled to attend a performance of acrobatics afterwards in the city. Safety in numbers, Felicia promised herself. She needn't share a table with Joshua again.

Dead wrong, as it turned out. When she entered the dining room it was to find nearly all her tour companions gathered around two large tables, and Maggie saving her a seat. Which left two at Felicia's other side empty. Those were the only chairs available when Joshua and Suzette entered together a little later, and Felicia watched with a sense of inevitability as he seated his companion and then took the chair next to hers.

'Hi,' he said in her ear.

Felicia half turned her head. 'Hi,' she acknowledged, and returned to studying the menu in front of her.

'Why don't we order a selection of dishes for the table?' someone suggested. 'We can all share, and have a taste of everything.'

After a minimum of discussion the plan was approved, and the menus removed.

The meal became a friendly free-for-all of passing, tasting, dipping and enthusiastic recommendations. Chopsticks were wielded with varying degrees of expertise and success, and as Felicia dexterously transferred a few pork balls from the serving dish to her plate Joshua commented, 'You're pretty damn good at that.' It had taken him several attempts to get a firm grip on one of the sauce-covered morsels.

'I often eat in Chinese restaurants.' She turned to Maggie. 'Would you like some of these?'

'If you'll kindly get them for me,' Maggie replied, waving her own chopsticks. 'I still haven't got the hang of these danged things.'

One of the children in the party, sitting on the other side of Maggie, piped up, 'You're holding them wrong. See, try like this!'

It was all very relaxed and sometimes hilarious. 'Group bonding,' Joshua murmured once, slanting a glance towards Felicia. 'How about it?'

'What?' She had to look at him, finding his eyes darker than usual, questioning her. Curious, perhaps.

'There was more than one wall out there today,' he said quietly, his voice covered by a burst of laughter from across the table as someone accidentally dropped a prawn into their drink. 'And this one's still intact.'

'I'm not sure what you mean.' Felicia looked down at her plate, toying with a grey, semi-transparent slice of sea cucumber and wondering if she really needed to eat it.

'We're all going to be together for a while, and a friendly atmosphere can help things along considerably. I thought last night...'

'What did you think?' she asked, more sharply than she meant to.

He was looking at her with a baffled expression. 'Was it the kiss?' he asked bluntly. 'Should I apologise?'

It had hardly been anything to make a fuss about, except for its unexpected effect on her. 'That's not necessary,' she said hastily. 'As kisses go, it scarcely rated, after all.'

A tight grin came and went on his mouth. 'Is that meant to be an insult?'

'I don't go around insulting perfect strangers.'

His brows twitched. 'Yow! A double whammy.' He glanced round the table. 'Look, it was an impulse, a nice way to end the evening, I thought. And...'

'And?' She looked up at him in challenge.

'And...I wanted to know whether you'd reciprocate. It seemed to me I had reason to hope for it. If I offended you, I'm sorry.'

'I'd forgotten all about it,' she assured him with spurious earnestness. 'It was totally unmemorable.' And she turned away to speak to Maggie.

She could feel him seething beside her, even as his deep voice answered something that Suzette said. Well, OK, she thought defiantly. He'd asked for it, and he'd got it—in spades. That should ensure that he stayed away from her for the rest of the trip. Only she wished she didn't feel so sick, as if she'd just done something peculiarly horrible.

Within days the tour group had developed a camaraderie that boded well for the rest of their time together. They'd visited temples and gardens, and most of them had ventured to the Chinese department stores and the street markets.

Joshua seemed popular, although when the group was taken to the Friendship Store where foreigners were encouraged to buy souvenirs, he had instead gone off somewhere on his own. Even Suzette didn't know where.

They were flown to Xian to visit the famous terracotta army and other archaeological sites, and travelled by rail and road to Qingdao on the Yellow Sea, through vast areas of cultivations and scattered pink-walled villages. Water buffalo plodded patiently along dusty raised roads by narrow canals, and in some places it seemed that the countryside had been unchanged for centuries.

Qingdao dispelled that feeling. A sleepy fishing village until only a hundred years ago, it was now a sprawling, traffic-ridden, skyscraping metropolis that Jen called '...a small city...only seven million people.'

Coming from a country that boasted a population of three and a half million or so overall, Felicia was unable to suppress a choked little laugh. Turning away to try and hide it, she caught Joshua's eyes, and an answering grin.

The first morning the group divided into those who wished to visit the Hi-Tech and Industrial Park and those who preferred a tour of specialty shops.

Relieved to find that Joshua had gone with the industrial tour, Felicia spent a relaxed morning with the bulk of the women browsing among a tempting array of embroidered silks, carved jade and cloisonné. It was difficult to limit her buying to a few irresistible pieces.

In the afternoon Maggie and several of the others declared they intended to spend the free time napping. Felicia welcomed the opportunity to take a walk on her own.

Strolling along the seaside promenade, where hundreds of Chinese holidaymakers and Japanese tourists enjoyed the broad beach a few feet below, she stopped to lean on the safety barrier, watching the swimmers and ball-players, and lifting a hand to her eyes to squint along the pier at the double-pagoda of the Rebounding Waves Pavilion.

Someone came to lean alongside her, and she felt the tightening of her skin that invariably told her when Joshua was near.

'Isn't this a bit silly?' he said mildly.

'What?' She lowered her hand but didn't take her eyes from the pavilion with the waves breaking gently around the rock on which it stood.

'Not speaking,' he said bluntly.

'I am speaking to you.'

'You avoid me at every opportunity.'

'Actually there aren't that many opportunities—'

The word *fortunately* hung in the air between them.

His hand on the rail beside her tightened. Then unexpectedly he laughed. Really laughed, with his head thrown back in genuine enjoyment. Watching him, she felt something clutch at her heart, and bit her lip, not wanting to recognise what had caused it.

The laughter was still in his eyes as he looked at her, shaking his head. 'You never miss a chance, do you? Why do I keep asking for it?'

'I've no idea.' Felicia straightened away from the railing and turned to resume her stroll.

'I don't believe that.' He was walking beside her. 'You strike me as a fairly intelligent woman.'

'Thank you. What does that have to do with anything?'

'Do I seem to you like the sort of man who enjoys hitting his head against a brick wall for the fun of it?'

'Since you ask...' Felicia allowed her voice to trail off delicately as she stopped to look at a display of freshwater pearls. Joshua shifted to stand half facing her.

The stall-holder smiled eagerly at Felicia. 'Hello, hello! Real pearl, very nice.'

'Very nice,' she assented, lifting a strand of the small, oddly shaped beads.

Joshua remained at her side. 'You want me to spell it out?' he asked.

'Are you a good speller?' Felicia asked coolly.

'Cheap,' the stall-holder said anxiously as Felicia let the strand of pearls drop from her fingers.

'Agreed,' Joshua commented, shooting him a brief glance. To Felicia he said quietly, 'I find you madly attractive, and I want to spend time with you. Now I'm wide open for the *coup de grâce*.'

'Only t'ree hun'red yuan!' the stall-holder offered, adding with hardly a pause, 'Two hun'red seven-five OK?'

Felicia said, 'I'm sorry, I'm not interested.'

'Two hun'red fifty!' the man offered as she began to move away. She smiled and shook her head.

'Not interested?' Joshua repeated softly. 'You were tempted, though.'

'Yes. I may change my mind later.'

'I live in hope.' There was laughter in his voice.

'I was talking about the pearls.'

'I wasn't, and you know it.'

She looked up, ready to deliver a stinging retort, let him know once and for all that she wanted nothing from him but to be left alone. With any other man it would have been easy. She'd have been polite, firm, unequivocal, trying to leave his ego intact while giving him a clear message that his advances were unwelcome.

But then she met Joshua's eyes and the words died on her tongue. He looked quite serious now, intense and determined, and she couldn't look away from the glowing amber depths. Her own eyes dilated, she could feel it.

He halted, moving half in front of her, oblivious of the people walking around them. 'What is it?' he asked her. 'You're not married, are you? Is there a man back home? Or has someone hurt you, made you afraid to step into the dark again?'

'None of the above.' With an effort she pulled herself together, forced herself to detachment. Perhaps she ought to claim a lover, a commitment. But instinct told her it wouldn't make any difference. 'I'm deeply flattered, of course, but—' She shrugged, not quite apologetically.

'You admitted you were tempted.'

'The pearls—'

'The hell with the pearls! You were sparring with me, and enjoying it, Felicia. Just as you enjoyed that kiss the other night.'

'You don't suffer from false modesty, do you?'

'You did reciprocate,' he reminded her. 'I wouldn't have done it if I hadn't fully expected you to.'

Unfair. And arrogant. He had no right to take her response for granted. But she could hardly deny that she had given it. 'A reflex. I was taken by surprise.'

Someone bumped against her, and Joshua took her arm and steered her away from the centre of the path to the side overlooking the beach. 'If you hadn't liked it your reflex would have been to pull away and slap my face.'

'Next time—' She stopped as a wicked grin curved his mouth. Fighting a shocking urge to laugh with him, she said, 'I thought you were telling me earlier that you're not a masochist.'

'Maybe I could learn. I've always enjoyed new experiences. A touch of vinegar can be quite refreshing after a diet of honey and sugar.'

'Suzette seems a nice girl.'

His eyes gleamed. 'Very.'

Genevieve had been nice—extraordinarily so. Had he found her cloying, become tired of her sweetness?

A shaft of pain and anger made her abruptly turn away, staring unseeingly at the tall buildings rising from the flat promontory at one end of the beach. 'I thought you were together.'

'No.'

'Suzette would like you to be.'

'Maybe. And maybe she deserves someone nicer than me,' he said.

'And I don't?' A dry note entered her voice.

'Probably.'

She turned to regard him curiously. 'So why should I be interested?'

'I haven't any idea, but I'm not imagining the signs.'

'Signs?' Her voice was frosty. He was so cocky, so convinced that she was attracted to him, when her feelings were much more complicated and much less complimentary than he had any idea of.

'I swear,' he said, 'that you know when I come into a room—even when you've got your back to the door. Your chin goes up and you get a little flush on your cheeks, no matter how carefully you're not looking at me. It has to mean something.'

It means I hate you. She wanted to shout it at him, right here in public, and walk away. Gripping the sun-heated railing, she looked away from him so that he wouldn't see that her eyes were hot with rage. He remembered nothing of that long-ago summer. Nothing about her, anyway. He couldn't, surely, have totally forgotten Genevieve?

'You watch me all the time when you think I'm not looking,' he said. 'The same way I watch you.' He paused. 'If you say so I'll walk away and not bother you again. But if you're going to do that I wish you'd tell me what it is you're afraid of.'

'I'm not afraid!' Her denial was instant and vehement.

'Well . . . that's a start.'

'I'm not afraid,' she reiterated, more to herself than to him.

She could tell him, get it all out in the open, watch his face when she revealed to him who she was. See him realise why she despised him.

Remember Genevieve? she'd say to him. Remember her little stepsister? The one who carried messages between you all summer? *Remember me?*

CHAPTER THREE

'THEN what is it?' Joshua was saying. 'Do you have some deep, dark secret in your past?'

He was smiling; it was a joke. *No,* she could have said, *but you do.*

She wondered how many other Genevieves had crossed his path, how many of them he'd loved and left. Now he was bored with women who fell at his feet too easily and was after more challenging game. Trying to avoid contact with him, Felicia had unwittingly piqued his jaded interest.

At least she'd have the petty triumph of turning him down flat. A small revenge for Genevieve.

Even as she opened her mouth to do it, the thought expanded, flowered in all its poisonous beauty.

Why settle for a small revenge? Why not play Joshua Tagget at his own game? String him along for a while and then dump him.

One part of her was appalled, but the idea was seductively simple. Her heartbeat increased, adrenaline fizzing under her skin.

In the extravagance of teenage grief she'd wanted to kill Joshua Tagget. Felicia knew now she was no murderer, but a more subtle vengeance was at hand. Didn't she owe it to Genevieve to reach out and take it?

'Felicia?' Joshua smiled, the same dazzling, irresistible smile she'd seen him direct at Genevieve all those years ago.

Surely she could make a pretence at liking him, at returning his interest, for a couple of weeks. For Genevieve's sake.

She smiled back at him, slow and mysterious. 'Of course I have secrets. Don't you?'

'None that matter.'

She kept the smile on her lips even as her blood simmered. *None that mattered.*

He deserved everything she intended to do to him. Everything. 'No wife tucked away in New Zealand?' she asked him.

'No wife, no ties.'

Leading a man on was dangerous, cruel and downright despicable. Usually. But this was different. This was for Genevieve, a belated reparation...

'What about Suzette?' she demurred with a twinge of compunction. The other woman had not exactly hidden her penchant for Joshua's company.

'I'm certainly not married to Suzette,' he said dryly. Momentarily he pursed his lips, as though searching for the right words. 'We found each other the night before the tour began, and had a couple of drinks together. She's very... friendly, and I try to be polite. I've never kissed her in the elevator—or anywhere else.'

'I see.' The relief she felt was absurd, and certainly inappropriate. For a moment her resolve wavered. What was she getting into here?

But she could handle it. She knew enough about him and was mature enough not to be misled again by shallow, facile charm and surface good looks. Deliberately, she flashed him a smile, and turned to walk on, tacitly inviting him to accompany her.

They strolled to the end of the promenade, and through a small park to a covered pavilion where they sat for a while enjoying the sea breeze, then retraced their steps back into the city.

Taking a different route to the hotel, they found themselves in the fish market near the old abandoned Catholic church. The smell was overpowering, but there was no doubt about the freshness of the produce. A good deal of it was still alive, including tanks full of hand-sized turtles or dark green frogs, and even a basin piled with soya bean worms.

'I expect they're delicious.' Felicia pulled out her camera and bent over to snap the fat, wriggling things.

'I'll buy you some if you like,' Joshua offered, digging a hand into his pocket.

'Thanks so much, but I wouldn't be able to cook them,' Felicia said regretfully. 'There are rules about that sort of thing in the hotel. Didn't you read the list of instructions from the Public Security Bureau?'

'Yes, I did. *All guests should come back to the hotel by 11 p.m.*'

'*Be courteous and civilised and keep the room clean,*' Felicia quoted, stopping to peer into a tank containing an enormous spotted sea snake. 'I think it's charming.'

'What, that fellow?' Joshua bent to examine the sluggish, sinuously coiled beast.

'The rules for guests.'

'Mmm, I've been in a few hotels around the world where I'd have liked someone to remind the guests about being courteous and civilised,' Joshua agreed. 'I was particularly taken with the one that says, *Hotel guests should live in the designated rooms and beds.*'

Straightening, he walked on a little further. 'What on earth are those?'

'Crabs,' Felicia decided as she moved closer to the deep containers. Each crab was tied with something that looked like twists of flax or rough twine, she supposed to stop them crawling away. 'Poor things.'

'You could say that about any creature destined for the pot. Do you like prawns?' Joshua gestured to a basket full of large pink crustaceans.

'I love them,' Felicia admitted. 'You're more of a white fish man, aren't you?'

'How do you know that?'

Her mind went blank, totally. She couldn't even recall how she knew, but the knowledge went back to the time when everything about him had seemed fascinating to her. She said, 'I . . . I remember you tucking into the fish at dinner the other night.'

'You do?' He looked surprised, then a smile tugged at his mouth. He thought she'd been watching him that closely.

'Yes. Oh, look—there's a shark. A small one.'

'It might be small, but I wouldn't care to encounter it in the water. Those are pretty impressive teeth!'

She'd been saved by his own conviction that she was attracted to him, Felicia thought. But she would have to be more careful.

Eventually they found their way back to the hotel, to find most of their party in the bar. Joshua got chairs for Felicia and himself and ordered drinks, casually throwing an arm over the back of her chair as they talked with the Australian couple and some other people. Suzette was at another table where some of the younger contingent had gathered. Felicia saw her direct a searching glance towards Joshua and note the position of his arm before turning away to talk to someone else.

You're better off without him, believe me, she mentally told the other girl. You don't know what bad news Joshua Tagget is.

Perhaps she should remind herself of that. At the fish market it had been fun bantering with him, and she'd almost forgotten that she was playing a part. Still, as long as she didn't lose sight of the main objective, that might not be a bad thing. She'd seem more natural and find the charade less of a strain.

As people began to drift off Joshua said quietly to Felicia, 'One of the contacts I met at the trade fair lives here. I'm having dinner with him and some other people, and he suggested I might bring a friend. Will you come?'

She would like to meet some Chinese people. And she ought to act eager to accompany him anywhere he wanted her to. 'Are you sure it will be all right?'

'Mr Lin was quite insistent that I was welcome to bring someone along. He's sending a car for me at six. Can you be ready then? I'll phone him and tell him there'll be two of us.'

She gave him her room number and he knocked on her door just before six, casting an approving glance over her short-sleeved blue dress. He was wearing a shirt and tie with dark trousers, and had a matching jacket slung over his shoulder.

'Is it formal?' she asked, wondering if the dress and the high-heeled sandals were too casual.

'I figured I'd best be on the safe side. If everyone is wearing suits I'll put on the jacket. You look fine,' he added, divining her concern. 'Cool and elegant.'

Their host arrived, dressed in a short-sleeved shirt worn loose over trousers. Joshua introduced them, and Mr Lin said, 'My wife is waiting for us at the restaurant. She will like to meet you, Miss Stevens. She is a teacher of English language at the university. She likes very much to practise her English.'

'Yours is very good,' she complimented him as he ushered them into his car, seating himself beside the informally dressed chauffeur. 'Did your wife teach you?'

'Some I already learn,' he said. 'But she...corrects my mistakes. So I get better.'

Mr Lin was a district inspector of agriculture, she learned. At the restaurant they were greeted by his wife, a pretty, round-faced woman, and introduced to three other men—two district officials and the manager of a peanut-packing plant.

The meal was served in a private room, and Felicia lost count of the dishes that were placed one after the other in the centre of the table. Mr Lin's wife occasionally dropped a special morsel onto Felicia's plate. Joshua slanted her an understanding grin as she concealed a fried insect of some kind beneath a little heap of leftover rice, unable to overcome her cultural bias even in the cause of good manners.

Their host got up to switch on the video player in one corner of the room, and the screen soon showed a man and woman wandering along a beach hand in hand, while Chinese words danced across the lower part of the picture.

'Do you like Karaoke?' their hostess asked Felicia as her husband picked up a microphone and began to sing in a tuneful baritone, soon joined by his wife's pretty soprano.

Hosts and guests took turns between courses to sing along to the video music. The factory manager performed a graceful regional dance, and before the end of the evening Joshua and Felicia were persuaded to perform, choosing a couple of pop songs and the New Zealand classics 'Pokarekare Ana' and 'Now is the Hour'.

The chauffeur dropped them back at the hotel before ten-thirty, and as the car drove away Joshua said, 'I don't know about you, but I need to shake that meal down. How about a walk?'

Gratefully, Felicia agreed. She was not only overfull, she also felt slightly muzzy from the pale local beer that had been liberally dispensed. Joshua had stood up well to the number of toasts that had been drunk, even though he had been expected to down an entire glass at each one, and there had been some hilarity and teasing among the men that easily breached the barrier of language.

People sat in lighted doorways playing card games or preparing food for the next day. On the corner a melon seller slept on a cot behind his piled wares, protected by a canvas awning.

'I hope you enjoyed your evening,' Joshua said.

'Very much.' Being with other people had made it easier, dissipating a little her consciousness of him sitting next to her. 'I liked Mrs Lin. She sings beautifully too.'

Joshua gave a small laugh. 'We didn't do too badly, ourselves, for an impromptu performance.'

'You carried me along. Experience counts.'

'Experience?'

She'd spoken without thinking again. She wasn't very good at this. 'Someone said you used to be in a pop group. Isn't it true?'

'In my misspent youth I played guitar in a band and did a bit of singing. The group only lasted for about a year before we broke up. We all had other interests to pursue.' He looked at her curiously. 'I don't recall mentioning it to anyone on the tour.'

'Not to Suzette?' Surely the woman had fished for some information about his past.

'Definitely not to Suzette. Who told you?'

Felicia shrugged. 'I can't remember. Did you make any recordings?' As if she didn't know.

'Only one. The uncle of one of the boys in the group arranged for us to record a few of our songs. The tape had a few airings on radio and then died.'

Genevieve had bought it though, and played it all summer, and she and Felicia had sung along to it. Felicia still knew all the words by heart. 'You weren't really famous?' she asked innocently.

Joshua shook his head and grinned. 'Yellow Fever was hardly a cultural icon.'

Felicia laughed. 'With a name like that, I'm not surprised.'

Joshua grinned. 'It's no worse than Pink Floyd. We thought it was pretty damn good, let me tell you.'

'You can tell me all you like. I don't have to believe you.'

'You think I'd lie to you?'

Oh, yes. For a few moments she'd almost forgotten. 'Don't all men lie to women?'

The smile on his lips changed, his look searching in the dim light. 'Not all men, no.'

He meant he wouldn't, and again the bitterness rose inside her. She wanted to confront him with his duplicity. Instead she said, 'Shouldn't we be heading back?

I wouldn't like to find they'd locked us out of the hotel if we're not in by eleven.'

He saw her to her room and waited for her to unlock the door. This time his room was located on the same floor as Felicia's, he'd told her.

'Thank you for coming with me,' he said.

'Thank you for taking me. I enjoyed meeting Mrs Lin and the others.' She turned to him. 'Goodnight.'

'Do you know, you've never called me Joshua?'

'Haven't I?' He was probably right. She hadn't realised she'd been avoiding it. 'Goodnight, Joshua.'

He bent forward quite slowly, so that she could have evaded his kiss if she wanted to. But she stood very still, mesmerised by the darkness in his amber eyes, the subtle scent of maleness that emanated from him.

His lips touched hers lightly, briefly—testing—then settled more firmly on her mouth, shaping it to his.

A door closed softly somewhere, and Felicia remembered who he was, where they were, and pulled abruptly away. 'We shouldn't...'

'The rules for guests don't say anything about goodnight kisses.'

'I don't think they're approved of in public, and I have rules of my own.'

'Really?' His eyes were enquiring. 'Such as?'

'Such as not offending people when I'm a guest in their country, for one thing.'

Joshua nodded. 'I'd go along with that.' He glanced along the corridor and leaned forward again, brushing another kiss against her lips. 'I hope that doesn't offend anybody.'

It should have offended her—repelled her, even. She should have been disgusted by his touch.

Instead, as she prepared for bed after closing the door on him, she was disgusted with her own weak-kneed response.

Next day they were taken to the Laoshan Mountains. The pure water that ran in the cold mountain streams was bottled for sale, and most of them had bought some of it to sip at during the heat of the day. Felicia shared a seat with Joshua as the bus wound up the steep road through a landscape like an ancient Chinese painting.

They alighted among clouds. Dark, twisted trees grew from crevices in sheer grey rock faces. In the restaurant where the party had lunch the sound of the cold clear mountain water cascading from high bluffs floated through the open windows.

They had half an hour after lunch to explore the area nearby, and Joshua suggested, 'Shall we see if we can get closer to the waterfall?'

A narrow path led to a view of the falls, a moving veil of white water sailing serenely over a cliff-face and into a large, deep green pool surrounded by smooth rock where plants clung and hung.

A group of Chinese returning from the water's edge were climbing an even narrower path punctuated by flights of steps cut into the rock. After they had passed, Joshua turned to Felicia. 'Want to go down?'

She was wearing sneakers with her light cotton trousers and a loose shirt. The ridged soles should cope with the sloping path quite safely. But when Joshua took her hand and led the way she didn't pull away from the strong fingers curled about hers.

The path wound about the cliff-face, sometimes shielded by overhanging trees. At the foot of it they were able to walk on a small grassy area and gain a new perspective on the falling water. Joshua removed his hand from hers, to rest his arm lightly about her shoulders.

A minute or so later something stirred her hair. There was no wind. Joshua had turned his head and was whispering, 'I want very much to kiss you.'

Her pulses throbbed, and her eyes stung with the effort not to look up at him and invite him to fulfil his wish. Schooling herself to indifference, she made to step away, but Joshua moved with her, then looked up. They could be seen from the top of the cliff.

His arm dropped and he took her hand again, pulling her with him under the shadow of the cliff and into a shallow cleft almost hidden by shrubby bushes. Leaning against the rock wall, he pulled her into his arms.

She told herself she went willingly because it was part of her plan, but her body curved to his as though it belonged there, and her arms slid about his neck without conscious thought. When his lips searched for her mouth she found hers parting eagerly, accepting his passion, returning it, sharing it. He tasted of beer and of him, hot and spicy and demanding. And it seemed as if he couldn't get enough of her, of tasting her in turn with his lips and his tongue.

His fingers buried in her hair, he tipped back her head and skimmed his open mouth across her cheek, along the line of her jaw and her neck, while his other hand left her waist to cup her behind, holding her against him.

Felicia gasped, gripping his shoulders to steady herself. And then voices floated down from the uneven steps above them and she stiffened, shifting her hands to his chest to push away from him.

Reluctantly Joshua lifted his head, his eyes brilliant and glazed, his cheekbones darkened with colour as he let his arms fall away from her. She saw him draw air into his lungs as if he hadn't breathed for seconds; she felt the same. Her knees trembled as she moved out of the rocky alcove and pretended to have been watching the water all the time.

She felt him come to stand behind her as the little party of Chinese tourists went past. Some smiled and looked at them with overt curiosity.

Joshua's hands found her waist in a gentle grip. 'They've guessed what we were doing,' he murmured. His fingers moved subtly, and she felt her breathing alter. 'I hope we didn't shock anybody.'

'Apart from me, you mean?' she asked involuntarily.

He laughed quietly. 'Are you shocked? You ain't seen—or done—nothin' yet!'

It was only a kiss, she reminded herself. Nothing to make a fuss about. But she was shaken at her own reactions, having serious doubts about the wisdom of her intentions regarding Joshua Tagget. If she didn't control her inconvenient sexuality better she could singe her fingers badly.

On the journey back to Qingdao she was so quiet that Joshua, enfolding her hand again in his as they crossed a bridge over a shallow river strewn with grey boulders, asked her, 'What's the matter?'

'I'm just fascinated by the countryside. Look, there are people swimming over there.' Downstream several young boys were splashing about near a small village built along the bank.

Joshua linked his fingers with hers and began stroking the back of her hand with his thumb. She didn't look at him, keeping her eyes determinedly fixed on the window and the landscape beyond it. But every nerve-ending in her body was aware of the tiny, insistent caress.

Genevieve, she reminded herself, gritting her teeth. Don't forget Genevieve.

As if she ever could.

They ate with others of the party in the hotel restaurant that evening. Later they were taken to a Chinese opera, and while she enjoyed the extravagant costumes and the traditional story, translated to them by Jen, the clashing cymbals that punctuated the performance left Felicia's ears still ringing after the tour party had returned to the hotel bar for a nightcap.

When Felicia said goodnight to everyone Joshua stood up too, and accompanied her to the elevator. She couldn't help noticing the covert glances from others in the party as they left.

He went with her to her door. She unlocked it and then turned to him, intending to say goodnight.

But she hadn't time to open her mouth before she found it captured under his, while his hand came up to cradle her head as he kissed her.

And just as she had that afternoon Felicia kissed him back, helplessly lost in a haze of desire. Until he manoeuvred them into the room and shut the door with his foot, then leaned back on it to draw her close against him, still kissing her.

The click of the latch penetrated the fog of heat and wanting, and Felicia made a sound of protest, pulling away from him.

For a second or so she thought he wasn't going to let her go, and a strange panic took hold of her. She pushed against him firmly, and broke free as his hold slackened.

'Sorry,' he said, sounding dazed. 'I suppose...you wouldn't ask me to stay?'

For a crazy moment she wanted to say, Yes, stay...please stay. She swallowed hard. *'Guests should live in the designated rooms and beds,'* she reminded him at last. 'You could get us hauled off to jail.'

'China has become much more liberal in the last few years. They're trying to encourage foreign visitors, for trade and tourism.'

'Still—'

'Yes, I know. You're right—I'm going.'

He opened the door, gave her a smile and said, 'See you in the morning,' before sauntering out.

What had she started? Felicia asked herself, sinking down on the bed. What had she got herself into, taking on Joshua Tagget? The man was lethal—in more than one way.

By morning she'd rationalised the situation. When she'd first met Joshua she'd scarcely known what sex was all about. With maturity her body was remembering the diffuse yearnings and moony dreams of her adolescence, translating them into adult and very specific desires.

With the emphasis on the physical. That was all this was, a powerful biological urge. No way could her mind agree that Joshua Tagget would fulfil all her needs.

No man was less likely to do that.

CHAPTER FOUR

BY THE time they arrived at Guangzhou everyone accepted that Joshua and Felicia were a couple. Suzette had flounced a bit for a few days but soon consoled herself with a husky Scandinavian who boasted a terrific tan and splendid teeth. He didn't speak much English but Felicia guessed that conversation wasn't a major consideration for Suzette at this point. His looks made him the ideal antidote for a woman's wounded ego.

Felicia didn't have to act as if she enjoyed Joshua's company, because however often she tried to remind herself that being with him was a means to an end, she was unable to keep that constantly in mind. She couldn't deny that he was a pleasant and stimulating companion, even without the added fillip of his physical attraction.

He was intelligent and sometimes funny, and in a discussion he was willing to listen to other views, including women's—which wasn't all that common among men in Felicia's experience. Always keen to learn about something new, he made heroic efforts to communicate with the Chinese when Jen wasn't there to translate. After one such encounter Felicia commented, 'I'm sure you've just done a lot to further the cause of international misunderstanding.'

Joshua grinned down at her. 'You're a nasty little cynic. We understood each other imperfectly.'

There were times when they exchanged a glance of mirth without needing to put into words what had caused it, or avoided each other's eyes for fear of laughing aloud. She found she was liking him far too much.

She even caught herself wondering if she'd been wrong after all about the events surrounding Genevieve's death. And that appalled her. What was she doing, trying to make excuses for Joshua when she knew there were none? She'd seen it with her own eyes, heard it from Genevieve's own lips.

She veered away from talking about her family, and Joshua gave her a thoughtful look once or twice, but didn't press the point. He didn't speak much of his own background, either.

As the bus speeded across the vast countryside towards Guangzhou and wound over hills, they had discovered similar tastes in art and reading, and found that they shared the wanderlust that infected many of their compatriots. She plied him with questions about the places he had visited in the course of furthering his business and exploring new markets and manufacturing techniques.

They talked and sometimes argued about the headline issues in the occasional English-language newspaper that someone managed to obtain and that was eagerly passed around among the passengers. The tour group had developed a community spirit of generosity and tolerance and good-natured teasing.

There were periods during the journey when Felicia and Joshua sat quietly without speaking, sharing a dangerous companionship while he held her hand in his against the warmth of his thigh. But it was physical attraction that had drawn him to her, and no doubt Joshua regarded this as a holiday romance that would fizzle out once they returned home. He was well into his thirties and had never been married—or so he said. He was probably accustomed to picking up women in his travels and leaving them high and dry. The thought made her throat hurt, and she had to remind herself yet again why she was with him.

Guangzhou, better known to westerners as the ancient trading port of Canton, was their last city. Here they were to stay at the White Swan Hotel for three days of sightseeing.

After dinner the first evening, Felicia and Joshua, with Maggie and a few others, sat at the huge windows in one of the lounge bars and watched the tourist ferries sail up the Pearl River. Later they strolled outside to admire the strings of lights that outlined the building and the swan emblem over the entrance. The gardens too were hung with lights, and as the others drifted off to bed Joshua held Felicia back with a hand on her wrist, drawing her into the seclusion of some shadowy bushes.

'Kiss me,' he said huskily, his arms sliding about her waist. 'I don't want to say goodnight under the eagle eye of a floor monitor or whatever they call them.' Every floor in the hotel had a smiling, uniformed staff member behind a small desk with a view of the corridor in either direction. 'I suppose if I persuaded you to let me into your room she'd come and fetch me out.'

Felicia smothered a laugh. 'I think their function is to help the guests, not spy on them.' There were no stern rules for guests posted in the rooms here. Guangzhou had hosted foreign visitors for nearly two hundred years, and she supposed its people were accustomed to differing standards of behaviour.

'Anyway,' Joshua's lips drifted along her cheek, 'I haven't kissed you all day, and I'm tired of waiting.'

Finally his mouth settled on hers in a questing, probing kiss.

A slow flame ignited inside her, and she breathed in the masculine scent of his skin, felt the hardness of his shoulder-blades as she slid her hands up his back, holding him. The kiss deepened and her head nestled into the cradle of his hand as his body curved over hers, her back arching against the warm, strong bar of his arm.

They'd kissed before, in snatched private moments that were rare and brief, but never quite like this. Desire ran through her like liquid fire, and she found herself opening her mouth to him while her body arched closer, until he made a low sound in his throat, and thrust a thigh between hers, swaying her off-balance as her knees gave way.

Shocked at herself, perilously close to losing control, she gasped into his mouth, and her hands scrabbled against his shirt in a feeble effort at repulsing him.

He lifted his mouth from hers, but instead of letting her go he held her snug against his thigh while he flexed it in a sensual, teasing movement.

She had to clutch at him to retain her balance, her breath catching sharply in shocked pleasure. *'Don't!'*

He had his eyes closed, his head thrown back slightly. 'Mmm,' he murmured deeply.

'Joshua!' Her own voice was husky, unlike itself. But while her body flowered with desire, craving this intimacy, her mind rejected him. Struggling at last in earnest, she hissed, 'Joshua, stop it! Let me go.'

His eyes opened slowly. She curled her fingers about his wrists behind her and tugged at them, and gradually his grip slackened. Finally she stepped free, but he grabbed her hand and pulled her back to him, this time

standing with an arm about her, his chin against her
temple. 'Just let me hold you for a minute. I guess I got
carried away. I'd like to make love to you right here,
right now. What about in Hong Kong? Can we get a
room together?'

He was taking a lot for granted. The thought steadied
her, and she worked on whipping up a feeling of indig-
nation to dispel dangerous temptation.

They had two more days in Guangzhou before
boarding a train to Hong Kong where they would take
their flights home. 'I don't know,' she said evasively.
'Let's...just see when we get there.'

'I want you.' His voice was stark, and he parted his
legs a little, pressing against her so she was in no doubt
that he spoke a literal truth. 'I'm going crazy with it.'

The shaft of triumph that shot through her was
mingled with panic and a sick dread. But this was just
what she'd been aiming for, she told herself resolutely.
If it came at the price of a little heartache—well, it would
be worth it.

She closed her eyes, her head resting on his shoulder.
'I'm glad you feel that way,' she said.

'Glad?' He groaned. 'You don't know what you're
doing to me, you witch.'

Oh, but I do! Felicia thought, assailed by trepidation
verging on despair. She knew because it must be close
to the same things he was doing to her. She reached up
to feather a kiss along his cheek, feeling like Judas.
'Won't it be all the better for waiting?' she whispered.

His answer was swift and wordless. He simply turned
his head and crushed her lips under another devastating
kiss. Only the sound of laughter and voices approaching
made him finally release her.

Felicia could hear the uneven harshness of his breath, and felt slightly dizzy herself as they broke apart.

She turned away from him blindly, making towards the safety of the brightly lit building. She must try to avoid letting him kiss her, he was much too good at it. Every time she went into his arms she came dangerously close to abandoning her plan and simply following her instincts.

Joshua captured her hand and held it in his until they had ridden up in the elevator, only then relinquishing his hold with a wry glance at the sleek-haired young woman who greeted them from her desk.

'See you tomorrow,' he told Felicia, his eyes lingering. She felt him watching her all the way to her door, his gaze drawing hers to him before she slipped inside the room. He looked taut and intent and unsmiling, but as their eyes met he lifted a hand and at last turned away.

The next day was a full one. Felicia was distracted from Jen's commentary by Joshua's light touch at her waist when they boarded the boat to cruise the Pearl River, by the warmth of his thigh against hers as the craft passed traditional sampans and motorised barges, by his fingers lacing into hers while they admired the glazed cobalt-blue gables of the Sun Yatsen Memorial, and his hand on her shoulder when they studied the striking amalgamation of eastern and western architecture at the Mausoleum of the Seventy-Two Martyrs on Yellow Flower Hill. Her physical delight in his touch only intensified the heavy feeling of guilt that nagged at her.

In the evening several of the party decided to make their way to the Cultural Park, and Joshua soon contrived to lose the others among the crowds enjoying en-

tertainments ranging from outdoor chess to roller-
skating. 'A great place for people-watching,' he said.
Glancing at a young couple walking by with linked
fingers, he tucked Felicia's hand into his own. 'Do you
want to visit the aquarium or have a look at the exhi-
bition halls, or...?'

'What about the outdoor theatre over there?'

They found seats and saw a frenetic play, solving the
language problem by whispering increasingly outrageous English dialogue to each other. Then they sat
in a secluded teahouse and drank *cha*, quietly talking.

'It's nearly over,' Joshua said, turning the small por-
celain teacup in his hands.

'Yes.' She was gripped with a peculiar mix of
emotions—nervous anticipation, dread, and a piercing
sadness. The sadness, she told herself, was for Genevieve.

'Felicia?' Joshua said very softly.

She forced herself to meet his eyes, hoping that hers
didn't betray the turmoil of her feelings. 'Yes.'

'One of my contacts arranged a meeting for me with
a man who runs an engineering plant near the city. He's
going to show me round tomorrow, give me lunch, and
hopefully we can talk business. I have to skip the tour
itinerary for the day.'

Felicia quelled a sharp disappointment mingled with
relief.

'I suppose you wouldn't care to come with me?'

'To an engineering plant?' Felicia repeated pensively.
More to dissuade herself than him, she went on, 'When
all Jen is offering is the Flower Pagoda at the Temple
of the Six Banyan Trees, the Park of the Stream of
Flowers, and the Tower Overlooking the Sea? When it

comes to agricultural machinery, I'm afraid I wouldn't know a cam shaft from a piston rod.'

Joshua cast her a grin, his eyes gleaming at her through lowered lids. 'I can't interest you in *my* cam shaft... or piston rod?'

Felicia nearly choked on her *cha*, but fortunately she wasn't required to answer because he went on smoothly, 'I could point out that according to our tour guide the Six Banyan Trees no longer exist.'

'The temple does. It's still used too.' Ruthlessly pursuing the change of subject, she added, 'Just think of how many people must have worshipped there over...it's about fifteen hundred years, isn't it?'

'Just think,' Joshua echoed dryly. 'Tomorrow night, then...? Could we sneak off somewhere together, just the two of us?'

'We can't do that,' she objected. 'The farewell banquet is tomorrow night.' Everyone they had spent the last few weeks with would be there, gathered in the big restaurant. 'I'll...I'll see you then.'

There was a moment's silence before Joshua said evenly, 'I suppose you're right. Maybe if you're in when I get back we could have a quiet drink before the banquet. I'll call your room, shall I? You can tell me all about what I missed.'

She managed a smile, a teasing rejoinder. 'Only if you promise not to tell me all about your cam shafts.'

He said, 'And I was kind of looking forward to it, too!'

They took a cab back to the hotel, but didn't go upstairs right away. Instead Joshua took her to the mezzanine floor, where they could overlook the indoor waterfall.

For a while they leaned shoulder to shoulder on a balustrade, watching the water splashing into the pool at the foot of a small pagoda lit by fairy lights, and the people crossing the ornamental footbridge from the ground-floor restaurant.

'It's so lovely,' Felicia said. 'I want to remember every detail.'

'Me too.' He had turned towards her, and when she looked back at him she was surprised at the intent expression in his eyes.

Their eyes locked for long moments before Joshua spoke again. 'Felicia—this isn't just a holiday fling, is it?'

Oh, no. It's much more than that. More than you have any inkling of. A familiar panic rose in her throat, born of her hopelessly conflicting feelings. 'Isn't it?' she said.

'Not for me.' She didn't fill the silence he left open for her, and he added, 'I hope not for you, either.'

Felicia swallowed. In that second she couldn't have spoken, even if she had been able to think of anything to say.

'Felicia?' Joshua said very softly.

She tried to look away, but his eyes compelled her. 'Yes?'

'I want to keep seeing you when we get back to New Zealand.'

He reached out and took one of her hands in his. 'We haven't even been to bed together,' he was saying, and her throat locked, her mind filling with erotic images. 'I was going to say it doesn't matter,' Joshua went on ruefully, 'but that's not true, because I do desperately want to make love to you. Only there's so much more to it than that. *You* are more to me than that.'

He can't mean it, Felicia told herself desperately. You *know* this man. He's just repeating things he's said to other women, hoping to inveigle them into his bed. Don't be stupid, don't make the same mistake that Genevieve did.

He said, 'It's the way you laugh—and the way you *don't* laugh sometimes when something's absurdly funny but you don't want to hurt a person's feelings by letting them know it. The way you handle a piece of art that you admire, with that utterly absorbed look on your face. And your clear-eyed way of cutting through claptrap to get at the heart of an argument.'

Felicia found her voice. This was safer ground. 'Some people would call that being simplistic.'

'No. It's being intelligent enough to see the tree instead of only the woods.'

'Thank you,' she said doubtfully.

'And,' he smiled at her and she felt as if he'd wrapped his arms about her, 'your caring heart.'

'My... my heart?' She tried to sound lightly sceptical, a little humorous, but it came out rather breathless.

'You worried some about Suzette, didn't you? You watched her like a mother hen for a few days. It was... touching.'

'Well, I had sort of...' Her voice trailed off.

'Taken me away from her?' he enquired dryly. 'As it happens, no. I was going to have to do something drastic and probably unkind if you hadn't come to the rescue.'

Felicia looked at him searchingly, and he sighed. 'She chatters. It was driving me nuts.'

'I'll remember not to chatter.'

A smile touched his mouth. 'You don't. And if you did...maybe it wouldn't make any difference after all. Just being you is enough.'

But you don't know who I am really, Felicia thought. You don't remember me. She looked down at their linked fingers and felt her eyes blur with tears.

He raised a hand and wiped a spilled droplet from her cheek. 'What is it, my love?'

'I...don't know what to say,' she whispered, stalling. But it was the literal truth. This sensitive, caring man couldn't be the unfeeling heartbreaker who had walked away from Genevieve when she needed him most. And yet...*I was there,* Felicia reminded herself fiercely.

'You don't have to say anything...or feel anything. I know we met less than three weeks ago, but we've been together every day, and not many people have that at the beginning of a...relationship. There've been lifelong friendships forged on this trip, I'll bet.'

That was probably true. A group of strangers, randomly flung together and forced to rub along, they had accepted one another's idiosyncrasies and enjoyed their virtues. Some had found soulmates. Pictures of children and grandchildren had been shown around, family stories shared, addresses exchanged, plans to visit made.

'If we didn't already live in the same country,' Joshua said, 'I'd have followed you home anyway.'

Genevieve, she thought, gritting her teeth and repeating the name in her mind like a mantra. Genevieve. Don't forget what happened to Genevieve.

She shook her head, blinking away the inexplicable tears. 'I want to go up to my room,' she said huskily. 'I...I need time to think. Please?'

'Sure,' he said almost instantly, turning to accompany her. 'I just didn't want you to imagine that in suggesting we share a room in Hong Kong I was only out for something light and temporary—"thanks very much, it was fun, and goodbye".'

She managed a jerky nod, some kind of smile. That was exactly what she'd expected him to want, exactly what she'd planned to refuse him at the very last. Now the moment was approaching and she was wavering, doubtful, bewildered.

The elevator they entered was crowded. A party of Japanese had evidently been having a night out, and they seemed to have enjoyed themselves hugely. Joshua stood with his hand on Felicia's shoulder.

'I'll see you to your door,' he murmured, his hand slipping to her waist as they left the elevator with several of the Japanese.

While the others dispersed, an elderly couple stopped at the floor steward's desk to make some enquiry, and Joshua guided Felicia down the corridor.

As she unlocked the door the steward went off in the other direction with the older couple.

Felicia made to turn to Joshua, to say goodnight, but he quickly increased the pressure of his hand and urged her inside with him, closing the door behind him.

'Joshua!'

'Too good a chance to miss.' He grinned. 'At least I can kiss you goodnight properly.' He wrapped his arms about her and proceeded to do so, his mouth both tender and urgent, coaxing her lips apart, persuading her body to fit into the curve of his, her head cradled snugly into the juncture of his arm and shoulder.

Her mind blanked out. They kissed for a long time, his mouth never quite leaving hers, altering from gentle to demanding, teasing to passionate. He traced the outline of her lips and tasted their inner softness, explored the warm, moist depths of her mouth with his tongue and then returned to soft, nibbling kisses, his lowered lids with their thick lashes flicking up now and then to see her reactions.

When he finally lifted his head his lips trailed hotly down the line of her throat, his tongue finding the small hollow at its base, lingering there with tantalising little thrusting movements. Felicia heard her own sharp, indrawn breath, and his low, purring laugh. 'I love you,' he whispered.

Her mouth parted in shock. *Love?*

His mouth covered hers again, taking her reaction for an invitation. Eventually they surfaced once more, and he inhaled against her cheek, deeply. 'Love your skin, your smell . . .'

'Scent,' she corrected huskily, distractedly. Her mind whirled.

This time his laughter was almost silent, but it shook his body, so closely melded to hers that she couldn't help but feel it. 'Scent,' he repeated. 'You *scent* of roses and moonlight and starlit water.'

Her answering laughter was breathless. 'You're a fool.'

'If you say so.' He wrapped her still closer, backing up to the door, and kissed her again, dropping his hands down her back, cupping and holding her with an explicit intimacy that set the blood roaring through her limbs as her mouth succumbed to the erotic assault.

One part of her was desperately reiterating that of course she didn't mean any of this, that she was going to send him away soon, thoroughly frustrated and acutely uncomfortable. But the soft, seeking aggression of his mouth and the feel of his strong male body against hers threatened to overwhelm all thought. She met the kiss with hungry eagerness, mindlessly responsive.

He released her mouth, flinging back his head, and emitted a low, anguished moan. His hands imprisoned her even more firmly as he made a slow, sensuous, explicit rotation with his hips. 'God, I can't stand this!' he said, dropping his head to look down at her. His eyes glittered and his face was dark with colour. His mouth looked softer, the lower lip full and sheened with moisture. She knew hers must look much the same.

Her heart pounding, Felicia felt her eyelids droop heavily, the lashes fluttering down to hide the answering brilliance of her own eyes. Daring to the point of recklessness, she allowed her lower body to mimic his movement, heard the quick intake of his breath, felt a shudder pass right through him.

Then his hands made a swift passage up her back, and he had her head between his palms and was kissing her again, this time with little gentleness but with stark, unrestrained passion.

The blood sang in her ears, and her arms hooked about his waist—to keep her balance, she hazily told herself, even as her mouth opened for him, accepted the hot invasion of his tongue.

She did need to hang onto him when he at last raised his head again, because now she was dizzy, her breath gasping as she let her forehead fall against the hard warmth of his chest.

His lips were probing the shallow groove below her ear. 'I love you, love you!' he breathed. 'I'm crazy for you, Felicia. Either send me away now, or hang the Do Not Disturb sign on the door and let me into your bed...into your body. Because I can't take this sweet torture any longer. And I don't have the strength to leave you of my own accord.'

The words made her tremble. Heat wove its way through her body to her face, burning her cheeks. *Let me into your bed...into your body.* She couldn't allow it...of course she couldn't. That would be nothing short of madness.

He dragged his mouth across her cheek, seeking her lips again, his kiss gentler now—persuasive, seductive. 'You taste so luscious,' he murmured against her lips, and his teeth nipped erotically at her lower lip. 'So good...I can't get enough of you. If it takes me a lifetime I'll never have enough of you.' He prised her lips apart again and bent her over his arm, while his other hand sought her breast and settled there, fitting his palm perfectly to the size and shape of it.

'A...a lifetime?' Felicia managed to stammer as his mouth moved to her cheek again, then slowly crept along the line of her chin. His hand stroked her breast, and she knew he felt her involuntary response when his palm shifted to cup the lower swell of it, while one finger explored that tell-tale hardness at the centre.

His voice unsteady, he said, 'You might as well know. I don't think I can live the rest of my life without you. Just give me a chance to make you feel the same way...please...darling?'

He stopped kissing her to look into her stunned eyes, and beyond the unmistakable heat of desire in the golden-brown depths she saw a blinding sincerity that staggered her. She'd never expected to see Joshua Tagget look humble, or so nearly afraid.

A surge of sheer primitive triumph in her feminine power momentarily swamped the physical sensations he was arousing with his caressing hands and the hardness and warmth of his body as it conformed to the contours of hers. She looked back at him with her eyes wide and dazed, and her lips parted on a low sound of astonishment.

He swooped, capturing them again in a kiss that seemed consciously restrained, full of both promise and pleading. Beyond the thunder in her blood one small part of her brain reminded her that she had him just where she had wanted him, almost begging for her to give in to him. And more than that, telling her that he wanted her not just for tonight, but forever.

She felt like a person literally split into two. Half of her was overwhelmed with the physical presence of the man who held her so tightly in his arms, whose kisses scorched her skin and turned her bones to liquid fire, whose touch was bringing her body to a fever pitch of desire. The other half reminded her that he was playing into her hands, exactly as she'd planned . . . and she tried to assess how to bring him to his knees.

And deep inside her a still small voice was saying: This could be your one and only chance. Whatever happens now, after Hong Kong you can never, ever see him, touch him, be with him again.

As if he'd sensed her indecision, he held her even closer, his mouth persuasive and possessive, until she tightened her arms about his neck, kissing him back with total abandon and an edge of something like desperation. Their mouths clung, clashed, drank in each other's taste, the scent of his skin filling her nostrils, the rasp of his incipient beard scratching her skin only adding an extra erotic charge to the kiss.

She felt him lift her until her feet left the ground, her flat Brazilian sandals slipping to the floor, and his legs parted, allowing her to wrap her thighs about one of his, her skirt riding up so she felt the hard muscular shape of him under the thin material of his trousers. He made a guttural sound in his throat, and then she abruptly pulled away, her feet once more on the ground.

'Stop,' she said. 'Joshua...let go.' She pushed her hands against his chest and he reluctantly released her, his eyes glazed, his laboured breath audible in the quietness of the room.

Her fingers fumbled with the door handle, and his breathing momentarily stopped, his eyes closing while his head jerked slightly to one side, as if he was in pain.

Almost leaning on it, because her legs felt as though they were made of candyfloss, Felicia opened the door a few inches. The small cardboard doorhanger swung on the handle against her fingers.

'All right.' Joshua opened his eyes. His voice was rough, slurred. 'If you want me to go...' Then he blinked, his whole body suddenly rigid with some kind of shock, his eyes following her every movement as she calmly removed the swinging sign from the inside of the door and hung it on the outside, then closed the door and deliberately locked it.

CHAPTER FIVE

SHE saw his chest rise and fall with the huge breath he took as his eyes returned to hers, a blazing question in them. Leaning back against the door with a partially appalled, partially exhilarated sense of having thoroughly burnt her boats, she gave him a slow, dazzling smile.

Her heart was jumping around like a cricket in a bottle, and she could scarcely breathe. *For God's sake,* some inner voice was screaming at her, *do you know what you're doing?*

Yes, she told it. I'm going to give him a night he'll remember all his life.

Joshua's hands were on her shoulders, dragging her to him. 'Thank you,' he breathed, and swung her right off her feet, taking the few strides over to the wide bed that the maid had already turned down on either side.

Almost reverently he lowered her body to the bed, her head resting on the cool, starched pillow. Something rolled softly away, and he picked up the tiny round package as he sat on the bed alongside her. 'Chocolate?' he asked, deftly stripping off the green metallic paper and poising the contents near her mouth.

She opened her lips and he dropped the chocolate between them.

As she bit on the sweet, mint-filled morsel he bent to remove his shoes and socks, then straightened and leaned down to kiss her, murmuring, 'Mmm, you taste delicious.' He sat up again and began unbuttoning his shirt, his smiling gaze holding hers.

Felicia watched, a peculiar fluttery feeling in her throat. When he had discarded the shirt on the floor he took one of her hands in his and placed her palm against his chest. His skin was warm and tanned and faintly furred with hair that tickled her fingers when he began moving her hand over it, his eyes closing as he breathed in deeply twice.

He opened them again, smiling tightly at her. 'Keep doing that, please,' he said, and he took his hand away from hers and began slowly to unbutton the soft silk blouse she wore with her cotton skirt.

She kept on stroking him while he divested her of both blouse and skirt, leaving her in a skimpy lace-edged bra and flowered panties. She felt the change in his breathing when she ran her thumbnail lightly across his flat male nipples, and when her hand reached the leather belt at his waist and she tucked two fingers down inside his pants.

He moved over her then, kissing her as though he couldn't wait any longer, and turned onto his back against the other pillow, bringing her with him.

There was another wrapped chocolate on it, and Felicia grabbed it as it fell to the sheet, moving away a little to unwrap it. 'My turn. Open wide...'

He smiled up at her and opened his lips, but only barely, so she had to push the sweet between them, and as she did so he captured her finger, drawing it into his mouth.

'You'll choke,' she told him, but he just made a muffled, indecipherable sound and began rolling the melting chocolate against the tip of her finger, and

stroking her with his tongue. His fingers found the clip
at the back of her bra and unfastened it, letting the straps
fall down her arms, her breasts freed to his hungry gaze.
He released her finger to rid her of the garment
altogether, then pushed her gently back against the pillow
and closed his mouth over one already pebble-hard peak.

She fancied she could feel the chocolate coating his
mouth and tongue, knew the taste of its dark sweetness
and sharp, cool mint was mingling with the taste of her.
The thought was madly erotic, and her hands involuntarily found his hair, her fingers threading through the
black strands to hold him to her, then drifting to his
shoulders as he lifted his head, smiled at her and turned
his attention to the other breast.

She tried to steady her breathing, to lie still and plan
how best she could drive him as wild as he was rapidly
driving her, but his mouth and tongue were doing such
wonderful, undreamt-of things to her that coherent
thought was becoming impossible.

At last he stopped, saying huskily, 'You taste wonderful.' He hitched himself up in the bed to look at her
face, but one finger was making lazy, tantalising circles
about the place his mouth had just left.

'Me...' Felicia murmured, smiling, '...or the
chocolate?'

He smiled back at her, his face close to hers. 'You
taste better...but the combination is irresistible. Pity
they only leave two.'

'I didn't eat last night's lot,' she whispered. 'They're
in the bedside drawer.'

'Oh, yes?' he drawled interestedly. His mouth came
down on hers, lingered, then lifted. With his eyes on her

face, he reached out a long arm, and she heard the drawer open and the small sounds as he fumbled around in it.

'Ah!' His hand came back holding another shiny little parcel. 'You open it,' he said, and passed it to her.

She peeled off the wrapping, then raised the chocolate to his mouth. He took it, but only to hold it in his lips, gently inserting the chocolate between hers, capturing it with his tongue to roll it against the roof of her mouth until it melted.

By the time it had, she felt as if she was melting too, into a hot, fluid mass of languorous desire. Joshua's hands were stroking her all over, shaping her hips and thighs and breasts, feathering up her inner arms, finding the smooth skin of her shoulders, the little hollows between the bones, then pursuing a wandering path downward.

His hand cupped the centre of her need, and suddenly focused it urgently, making her press against him, gasping. She bit at his shoulder, tasted the saltiness of his skin, and her fingers raked through his hair, drew his head down to meet her mouth with his.

She discovered the groove of his spine, and ran her fingers down its length, only to be frustrated by the trousers he still wore. Impatiently she found his belt buckle and tugged the tongue of leather from its fastening.

He shifted away from her, grinning as he helped her, then stood up to shed the garment along with his underpants, pausing to take something from his trouser pocket. He slipped the flat little packet under the pillow and lay beside her, gathering her back into his arms and stroking her again. 'We have one chocolate left. Do you have any ideas for it?'

Give him a night to remember, her alter ego exhorted, reminding her. 'I might have,' she said, and stretched against him. He touched her again as he had before, and the pounding excitement wiped away her brief misgiving. She whispered in his ear, and he laughed quietly, pretended shock, and then dipped his head to kiss her throat, her shoulders, her breasts, and places so intimate and unexpected that she felt her breath stop in her throat.

She touched him in return, and kissed and caressed and used her teeth and tongue, her fingers and her toes, prolonging the exquisite agony with bold advances and teasing retreats, hot and hungry and then slow and sensuous, until he was trembling in her arms, his breath coming in great uneven gasps, and he finally said raspingly, 'Enough, darling! I can't . . . hold out any longer. Please.'

She let him smooth her panties down her legs, and run his hands between her thighs and part them, and touch her tenderly with a series of silken strokes before he slid his hand under the pillow, and after the briefest pause made himself mysteriously, intimately one with her.

All her senses coalesced in a seething whirlwind of vivid, spinning sensation, centred on the joining of their bodies, on the overwhelming musky beauty of his skin gliding against hers, the strength of the arms that held her so securely when the world seemed about to slip away, on the unequalled closeness that was the right of lovers who trusted each other and had committed their lives to each other's care. And in one lucid, crystalline moment before she was swept away into the shuddering, pulsing vortex, her mind spoke clearly and unnervingly. *What have you done?*

* * *

Joshua kept her in his arms all night, sometimes in renewed passion, sometimes in abandoned, replete sleep. At dawn he kissed her awake, and made love to her yet again with exquisite finesse, paying homage to her body with delicate touches, lingering kisses, and finally deep, urgent thrusts that brought her to a shattering, explosive climax.

Afterwards he held her for a long time, only drawing back when he felt the dampness of her tears against his bare chest.

'What?' he asked her, his brow furrowed with consternation. 'What is it? I didn't hurt you...?'

Felicia shook her head. Her emotions were so excruciatingly muddled she couldn't have explained even if she were willing to. She wanted to stay in his arms forever, it felt so right to be there, and yet she was conscious of a growing sense of wrongness, like a minuscule lump somewhere near her heart that passion and its aftermath of delicious lassitude had kept at bay, but that now was growing bigger by the moment, hard and hurting, and threatening to burst free and break her into little pieces.

Last night she'd had a strange feeling that there were two separate beings inside her skin. Which one had made the fateful decision to welcome Joshua Tagget into her bed—the breathless, passion-thralled woman who turned to living, breathing flame in Joshua's arms, or the vengeful angel of destruction?

What difference did it make? The stakes were higher now. The denouement when it came would be all the more shattering. That was what she wanted, wasn't it?

Her heart faltered at the thought, and her temples went cold. Everything in her recoiled. I can't do it, she realised. I can't. I never meant it to go this far...

But if she didn't follow through, her surrender had been pointless.

Look at you, a jeering inner voice sneered. Even now you're tempted to forget why you did it and wallow in the pleasure he can give you.

'Felicia?' Joshua was looking at her with concern.

'It's all right,' she managed to gulp out. 'I'm just... never mind.'

'But...' His thumb stroked away the salty trickle. 'Tell me.' He bent and kissed her damp cheek. 'I've never made a woman cry before,' he murmured, an anxious smile quirking the corner of his mouth.

So casually delivered, the remark was like a shower of ice. Even if he hadn't seen Genevieve's tears, he couldn't have been blind to how she'd felt about him. He must have known what his callous rejection had done to her.

Felicia's spine stiffened and her teeth involuntarily clenched. She had a mad urge to tear herself from his arms, to hit him, to scream.

And cry. Most of all she wanted to cry—not the quiet weeping of despair, but wrenching, howling sobs of grief and rage.

She swallowed it all down. 'Never?'

Joshua didn't seem to notice the coldness in her voice. He laughed softly, but behind the laughter the concern was still there. 'I don't go around hurting women.'

She wanted to believe him. But she knew it wasn't true. It wasn't true, only...

Was it possible he hadn't known how Genevieve had felt about him?

She'd discovered them one day locked in a passionate embrace in the sandhills backing a secluded part of the

beach. Genevieve's discarded bikini top lay caught on a
bunch of spinifex beside them, and Joshua wore only a
pair of hip-hugging swim briefs. His head was bent as
he kissed her throat, and Genevieve's was flung back,
her eyes closed, a taut longing on her face. They hadn't
seen Felicia and she'd backed off down the sand-dune
behind her and run, the scene etched in her mind forever.

And once she'd heard scuffling noises in the kitchen,
Genevieve's soft laughter cut abruptly off to be followed
by silence and then Joshua's low, driven voice. *'I love
you!'* And Genevieve's long, breathless sigh. 'Oh,
Joshua, my sweet, sweet Joshua! Tell me again!'

Felicia stirred against his shoulder. 'I can't be the first.'

He tried to look down at her, but she dipped her head,
avoiding his eyes. 'Far as I know,' he said.

'You've never loved a woman—or made her love
you—and left her?'

'No.' He lifted her face and his lips pressed fiercely
on hers, and then softly touched her cheek as if to make
up for the fierceness. 'No.'

Liar, she thought, with a vast, distant, numbed
sadness. All her righteous anger had died away.

She tried to say Genevieve's name, but something
seemed to block her throat, choking back the one word
that would change everything.

Maybe he didn't even remember Genevieve. Maybe he
wouldn't remember Felicia either, twelve years from now,
despite what he'd said last night. Men would say anything to get a woman into bed. Some of them even meant
it at the time. Was that what it had been like with
Genevieve? Perhaps he had thought he loved her, until
she asked for a commitment. And then he'd backed off,
run away, left her without anyone to turn to.

There were no excuses for that.

She found herself putting off the moment of truth. There's no hurry, she told herself. I need to think.

'You have to go.' She forced herself to sit up. Impossible to expect any intelligible thought while he remained here in her bed, holding her like this.

He lay on the pillow, looking up at her, one hand lingering on her cheek. 'I don't want to leave you.'

'You can't stay here all day. The floor steward will guess where you spent the night.'

'I think they change shifts early in the morning. With any luck your reputation will remain intact.'

'Still...' she said, trying to sound crisp and dismissing.

'Yes, all right. I'll leave.' Sitting up with obvious reluctance, he pressed a light kiss on her unresponsive lips, drew back with a quizzical look, and sighed, then threw off the covers.

'Shall I cancel my appointment?' he asked her as he slipped into his clothes. 'We could slope off somewhere, spend the day together.'

'No, don't do that,' Felicia answered quickly. 'You can't afford to offend a business contact.'

He was probably waiting for her to say she had changed her mind about accompanying him, but she direly needed time away from him to take stock of the situation. Increasingly, she was horrified at her recklessness of the night before.

'Regrets, Felicia?' Joshua looked down at her, a small frown remaining between his brows. 'If you're worried that I'll take too much for granted, you needn't be. I did notice that you haven't said you love me. But there's time...plenty of it.'

Very little, in fact, Felicia argued mentally, but not aloud. Instead she tried to smile.

He seemed to hesitate, then said regretfully, 'There's a car coming for me at nine.' He dropped to the bed, touched her hair, and bent to brush the lightest of kisses against her lips. 'See you tonight,' he said. 'Think of me, OK?'

Felicia scarcely thought of anything else all day. She'd felt increasingly sick with a combination of fear and despair and a wrenching sense of guilt that no amount of justifying her actions was able to dispel.

What have you done? The question that had been swamped, overwhelmed, drowned by passion and specious logic last night returned to haunt her, and clamoured in her mind while she showered and changed for the farewell banquet.

A long time ago she had learned that lust was no substitute for love. These days she never let it overcome her better judgement.

Nor had she now, she tried to persuade herself. She had been thinking of Genevieve.

For about two minutes! her conscience unrelentingly accused. After that you just closed your eyes and enjoyed every minute...every second.

She'd let Joshua's potent sexuality drown her misgivings, erase from her consciousness the only valid reason for their being together in any way at all.

Face it, you wanted him. You've wanted him since you were thirteen years old, and you made Genevieve an excuse to sleep with him—

No! It wasn't like that!

Yet even this morning, instead of telling him she had been stringing him along and had no intention of sharing a room with him in Hong Kong or anywhere, she had weakly let things lie, delaying the inevitable showdown.

Without his presence, his kisses and the lambent fire in his eyes to arouse her body and muddle her thinking, what she had done looked more and more like a despicable, self-serving act of betrayal, only made worse by the feeble pretence that she'd been pursuing her original intention of exacting an eye for an eye, atonement for Genevieve's poor, pathetic, wronged ghost.

Despite the heat of the sun, scarcely dissipated by the broad awnings that shaded the city's main streets, or by the trees in the extensive park surrounding the Tower Overlooking the Sea, as the hours dragged by she grew inwardly colder and colder.

Trailing about with the others while Jen expounded on ancient buildings and art treasures that would normally have enthralled her, she scarcely heard a thing. Her mind relentlessly replayed the events of the previous night, recalling every word, every nuance of Joshua's voice.

She wanted desperately, shamingly, to believe in him, in his implicit promises of a future. But even if she dared trust his word, there could be no future for them. The memory of Genevieve would always stand between them.

As she pulled fresh undies from a suitcase, her nerves were jumping so badly that she seriously contemplated pleading sickness and not going down to the banquet at all. The phone burred, and she stood still, holding her breath until at last the sound stopped.

Coward, she told herself, dragging out of the wardrobe the first thing that came to hand—a cool, low-necked cotton dress patterned with forget-me-nots. Very suitable, she thought grimly, tugging it on. She thrust her feet into sandals and turned to the mirror to make up her eyes and apply a dash of lipstick.

She should have picked up the phone and told him lightly, as though it didn't matter, that she'd made a mistake last night, that he was no longer welcome in her room, in her bed, her life. 'It was nice but it's over.'

She capped the lipstick and put it down, wondering how Joshua would react to that. He'd be surprised, disbelieving, perhaps angry.

And if he'd meant any of what he'd said last night, profoundly hurt.

Yes. That's what you want, isn't it?

Was it? She was no longer sure—of anything.

Would Joshua even care? If he was the shallow, manipulative bastard she'd thought him, then so far as he was concerned he'd had one night of lovemaking with a woman he'd known for a little less than three weeks. He'd maybe suffer a momentary pang or two of disappointment, then he would shrug it off and move on to his next trip, his next brief affair.

And if he wasn't like that? If all he'd said last night was true...

He said he loved me.

He'd told Genevieve that too. And how many others in between? A lot, probably, in twelve years.

Remembering his tenderness when he'd touched her last night, made love to her, she was assailed by doubt. Could she be wrong about what had happened that summer so long ago? But her memory of events was as clear as if they had taken place yesterday, and there was no escape. Some things were impossible to forget.

Genevieve had believed in him. She'd been prepared to give up everything for him. But when she appealed to him to take her away as he'd promised he simply abandoned her. And after that defection she'd seen only one way out...

Always Felicia came up against that, and here memory merged into nightmare. Her temples dewed, and nausea rose in her throat.

It was almost time to go to the dining room. Cravenly she had left it too late to join Joshua for drinks beforehand.

If he looked at her the way he had last night, touched her that way again...

You've let him get to you, she told herself, viciously pulling a comb through her hair. He's mesmerised you, just as he did Genevieve. You fool. What the hell possessed you last night? All that crap about setting him up—what a pitiful excuse.

Her face was pale. She hunted for some blusher and stroked it across her cheekbones with a brush.

But...last night she'd been sure his feelings were genuine.

All the better, said the hard, bitter, vengeful part of her that remembered Genevieve, while the treacherous part of her that forgot everything else whenever Joshua took her in his arms went soft with longing.

By now most of the party would be in the bar having pre-dinner drinks. Joshua would be looking for her...waiting. And later he would want to come with her to her room.

Her body throbbed with wanting, just at the thought of his touch. She looked into the mirror and found her eyes shadowed with pain.

Determinedly her lips compressed. *You started this. Finish it!*

Where would she ever get the courage to do it? He only had to look at her and she was lost.

If you don't do this for Genevieve you'll never be able to look yourself in the face again. What kind of sister are you? Sleeping with Joshua Tagget, letting him use you as he used her—you've made her memory a pretext for giving in to your own raw lust for the man who caused her death.

Oh, God. She shuddered. 'It isn't true,' she whispered. 'It wasn't like that!'

With some faint hope that she wouldn't have to sit beside Joshua, Felicia entered the dining room late. But of course he had saved her a chair next to his, and no one minded. In their eyes he and Felicia belonged together, just like Suzette and her Scandinavian, and a few others who had paired off during the tour.

The banquet dishes looked and smelled delicious, but Felicia toyed with tiny morsels, barely managing to swallow anything. Joshua talked to her in low, lazy tones, and she scarcely heard what he said, answering automatically. Once he asked if she was tired, and she hesitated, then grabbed the excuse. 'It's been a hectic three weeks. It's starting to tell on me.'

Three weeks, she thought bleakly. In so short a time could a man like Joshua, handsome and successful and uncommitted at past thirty-five, have really fallen in love with someone he didn't remember ever knowing?

Or, more likely, could such a man have perfected a technique for persuading attractive travelling companions to sleep with him?

Objectively there was no doubting which was the more plausible. She swallowed a few grains of rice and felt as though she might choke on them. There was no escaping the distinct possibility that she'd been thoroughly hoist with her own petard, caught in the trap she'd laid for Joshua. He would probably remain unscathed, but her heart was being torn in two.

The man at her other side was speaking to her, she realised, and she tried to listen, turning her gaze to him and forcing a polite smile to her lips.

' . . . a great tour. My wife and I have been all over the world, but this has been something different. Let me pour you some of this rice wine. It's got quite a kick to it, let me tell you.'

'Thank you.' But while she chatted to the man and answered remarks from others across the table she was acutely conscious of Joshua's hand lying on the table-cloth only inches away, of the warmth and subtle male fragrance emanating from his body.

To distract herself from the unbearable, scorching awareness of it, she said randomly to the guide, 'Joshua took me to a banquet with some local people in Qingdao—all evening they were drinking toasts to each other. Is it customary in China, Jen?'

The woman nodded. 'This is very much done in China, many toasts proposed during the meal.'

Almost immediately one of the young men bounced to his feet and proposed a toast 'To Jenny, the best and prettiest guide in all China.'

Soon people were bobbing up and down all around the table between courses, proposing toasts to China, to their various home countries, to each other. One went to the middle-aged man who was voted 'class clown' and one to a motherly elderly woman who had become 'Gran' to them all.

The meal was almost over. A whole fish was served on a bed of rice, the dish symbolising, Jen said, 'peace and more than plenty.'

A middle-aged man rose to his feet beside his blushing wife and announced that in two days' time they would celebrate their thirtieth wedding anniversary. Almost overcome with emotion, he smiled down at the plump, greying woman beside him, taking her hand in his as he touched his glass to hers and said, 'To love that lasts a lifetime.'

Maggie wiped away a tear before joining in the toast, and the whole table gave their well-wishes to the happy couple.

Joshua turned to look into Felicia's eyes, lifting his own glass.

She couldn't tear her eyes away from the glow in the dark gold depths of his. A huge lump in her throat prevented any response. Her temples pounded. She closed her hand about her glass, which had just been refilled with clear, potent rice wine, but it might have been made of lead.

Somehow she forced her gaze away from him to the anniversary couple, lifted her glass and took the merest sip. Her other hand lay on the tablecloth beside her plate, and Joshua put his over it, capturing her fingers.

The gesture recalled with astonishing vividness a day years ago: she'd been lying on a blow-up mattress on the deck outside the upstairs living area of Genevieve's house, pretending to read a book while she surreptitiously looked her fill at Joshua Tagget pushing a noisy motor mower around the lawn, his chest bare and brown, glistening with a light film of sweat above faded, hip-hugging jeans tucked into a pair of rugged workboots.

Genevieve came out of the house bearing a long glass of beer, the amber liquid glinting in the sun, a white layer of foam frothing on top. She gracefully crossed the new-mown grass, a semi-transparent white cotton dress swirling about her legs. And Joshua turned his head and stopped the mower, pushing down the protective ear-muffs he wore to lie on his neck, while he watched her walk the last few yards towards him.

In the sudden silence Felicia had heard clearly the muffled thump and shush of the waves on the unseen beach, the distant shouts of children, a crying gull. Genevieve held the big glass with both hands and gave it to Joshua, lifting her face to watch him as he took it and thirstily downed the beer, one hand still on the handle of the mower.

He'd passed the emptied glass back and grinned down at her, and they stood talking for several minutes. The words weren't audible on the deck, but Genevieve's cheeks were delicately flushed and her eyes soft with secrets as they spoke. Then she put her hand briefly over Joshua's where his fingers curled about the handle of the mower, and turned to go back to the house. Joshua watched her all the way, his face tense and hungry, only bending to restart the mower after she had disappeared inside.

Felicia remembered that look as if it were yesterday.

Joshua's hand now burned on hers as he laughed across the table at something Suzette's Scandinavian was saying in his heavily accented, laboured English. His fingers tightened slightly, as if he'd felt her chilled, in-stinctive urge to recoil from him.

Do it now! her mind commanded. If you let him come back to your room again, you know he'll kiss you and touch you and you'll lose your mind, you want him so much.

And then one day he'll turn his back on you, just as he did on Genevieve, and where will you be then?

Adrift with bitter memories and a guilty conscience.

He was saying something now to Suzette, smiling across the table, but his hand still imprisoned Felicia's.

He turned to meet her concentrated stare, and the laughter faded from his face. 'Felicia?'

Felicia pulled her hand away from the light, firm pressure of his. Her heart pounded uncomfortably; her whole body felt hot, but weightless. In that moment she saw with sickening, cold clarity the only sure way to avenge Genevieve and irrevocably end this bitter charade.

She pushed back her chair and got to her feet, feeling as if she were performing in a dream, a nightmare. Joshua moved his chair too, to watch her with smiling curiosity.

As she stood there, silently waiting, the table hushed expectantly.

Her fingers tightened on the glass she held.

'To Joshua,' she said huskily but with perfect diction, 'without whom this trip wouldn't have been nearly so enjoyable.' She sought his eyes. 'And... last night you made it even better.' She smiled, although she had never felt less like smiling in her life. There was a buzzing in her head, and she was sure her cheeks had paled despite the warmth of the room.

Joshua smiled too, a surprised but tender smile. The tenderness almost made her resolve falter and she had to pause, momentarily clenching her teeth. Ignoring the suggestive guffaws and gleeful hoots from some of the men, she added, 'It's been a giggle, Josh, and that was the best joke of all. I haven't laughed so much in—oh, ten years or more.' Flinging his own words in his face, she went on, 'But everything comes to an end, doesn't it? So...thanks very much, it was fun, and...goodbye.'

It was as if a hand had passed across his face, wiping it of all expression. His eyes were abruptly lifeless, his features stone-like. Felicia lifted her glass quickly and emptied it, welcoming the eye-watering bite of the potent liquor, then sat down.

A couple of people made sounds of mock-commiseration, then someone laughed uncertainly and raised his glass, followed by others. Peripherally Felicia was aware of Maggie across the table giving her a puzzled look, and of several covertly inquisitive, curious glances darting between herself and Joshua, but her eyes were fixed on the tablecloth before her, while he sat perfectly still, a hand curled hard about his glass.

Someone proposed a toast to a safe journey home for them all, a chorus of agreement broke the spell, her neighbour refilled Felicia's glass and she wrenched her gaze away from its mesmeric fixation.

The evening was nearly over, thank heaven. She felt drained, and curiously ashamed, sick to her stomach and in need of a good weep.

The last dishes were being cleared from the table, and Joshua abruptly stood up. 'I want some fresh air,' he said. 'Excuse me. Felicia—come with me?'

His eyes were so hotly compelling she nearly obeyed their silent message, but after swallowing painfully she managed a casual, 'Not tonight, thanks. I need to pack for tomorrow.' She was lying and he knew it, but in front of all these people there was damn-all he could do about it.

His mouth tightened, his eyes going dark and angry, and Felicia almost expected him to bend down and haul her bodily from her chair. But after a second or two he gave a jerky, ironic nod instead and strode out of the dining room.

Others reluctantly began stirring to leave, and Maggie slipped into the vacant chair beside Felicia. 'Are you all right?' she asked.

'I'm fine.' She had done what she'd set out to do, hadn't she? Vindicated Genevieve's memory and exacted a just retribution. So why didn't she feel good about it, about herself? Why did she have this dreadful hollow feeling inside as if she'd done something horribly wrong?

'Did you and Joshua quarrel?' Maggie asked diffidently.

'No, of course not. He just wants a walk in the garden and . . . I don't.'

'Mmm. I didn't mean that, exactly. You two seemed so . . . suited. I really thought, as you both come from New Zealand . . .'

'Holiday romances don't last.'

'Sometimes they do . . . if you give them a chance. I'd have guessed Joshua was quite serious about you.'

Felicia shook her head, managed a bitter smile. 'Joshua's not the type to be serious about anyone, Maggie.'

'Are you sure? Oh, I'm sorry. It's none of my business, I just like to see people happy.'

'I'm happy.' Felicia gave her a wide, empty smile.

'And Joshua?' Maggie enquired gently.

'Joshua's a big boy,' Felicia reminded her, hardening her heart. 'I don't think you need worry about him.'

On the train Felicia slipped into a seat next to Maggie. She knew when Joshua brushed by them, through that mysterious intuition that infallibly told her he was near. Maggie glanced up, then turned her gaze for a few moments to Felicia, but said nothing.

The journey seemed interminable, but at last they drew up in the noisy, dusty railway station at Hong Kong and alighted with their bags. Some people were off to the airport that day, others had taken the option of being booked into a hotel in Hong Kong for the night. A minibus was waiting outside.

Felicia swapped addresses with a couple of people and by the time she boarded the bus Joshua was already there, sharing the back seat with two other men. She took one at the front, and was relieved when Suzette slid in beside her, looking slightly red-eyed and with her mouth denuded of her usual bright lipstick. Her Scandinavian had departed to catch his flight home.

'Did you give him your address?' Felicia asked.

Suzette nodded. 'But he can't write in English.' She sniffed forlornly. 'I don't suppose we'll ever see each other again.' She looked around the bus. 'You're not making up with Joshua? You really *were* dumping him last night? But I didn't believe you meant it.'

'Didn't you?' Joshua had certainly been in no doubt. He still didn't know who she was, and there was no need now to tell him; so he would see no reason for her brutal rejection other than his own inadequacy. The avenging angel who had possessed her last night would have said that he deserved to be haunted by the thought. Today that transcendental being of fiery righteousness seemed to have deserted her, and there was only a small whimpering creature deep within her heart keening, *What have I done? What have I done?*

'What did he do to you?' Suzette asked.

'It's a long story.'

'Well, it can't be that long,' Suzette reasoned, 'if you only met him three weeks ago.'

'True.'

'I don't follow...'

'Never mind, it doesn't matter.'

'He looked pretty stunned last night.' Her sideways glance might have been censorious, but also slightly awed. 'I don't think I could do that to a man.'

'It wasn't easy,' Felicia muttered. Her stomach still curdled when she remembered it. She turned to gaze unseeingly out of the window at the passing traffic.

'You seemed as if you'd known each other forever. Actually, at first I was pretty keen on Joshua myself,' Suzette added as if it was bound to be news, 'but he hardly ever took his eyes off you long enough to even see me. It was pretty frustrating, let me tell you.'

Felicia flashed her a wry smile. 'Sorry.'

Suzette shrugged. 'That's OK. It's a shame things didn't work out for you.'

'Thanks, but don't waste your sympathy on me—or on Joshua. We both knew what we were doing.'

After she'd signed in at the hotel and been taken up to her room, Felicia left her bags on the luggage rack and crossed to the window. It was windy outside; palm trees along the roadside tossed and swayed, and the sky was overcast. From here it looked cold and bleak, but people in the street wore short-sleeved shirts, summer dresses. Inside, the air-conditioning kept the room temperature down, raising goose bumps on her arms, while outside was like a warm, damp oven.

She rubbed her arms and turned away. Tomorrow morning she'd be flying home. For the rest of the day she intended to explore Hong Kong.

And of course that had nothing to do with avoiding Joshua.

It was bad luck, though, that when she arrived back with a bulging carrier bag she bumped into him and Suzette leaving the hotel.

Suzette, her arm hooked into Joshua's, brazened it out. 'Hello, Felicia,' she said brightly. 'We're just going to find some nice place for dinner. Been shopping?'

'Mmm-hmm.' She'd found it difficult to work up any enthusiasm, but now she was glad she had forced herself. 'I've had a wonderful time.' She indicated the carrier bag, flashing a completely false smile in Suzette's direction, evading Joshua's gaze.

But he suddenly spoke. 'What are you doing about dinner?'

Astonished, she glanced at him then. She couldn't tell anything from the controlled rigidity of his face, but his eyes were scorching. Hastily she looked away. 'I'm not very hungry,' she said.

'You could come with us,' Suzette offered.

Felicia's smile warmed. 'Thanks,' she said with sincerity, 'but I'll pass on that. Enjoy yourselves.' And she turned towards the elevators, not looking back to watch them leave together.

CHAPTER SIX

IN THE morning Felicia packed quickly and then went down to have breakfast. When she got back the message light on her telephone was blinking.

Joshua?

Her heart did a strange revolution at the thought, her body growing hot all over, then cold.

She picked up the receiver, and was told her message was from Miss Suzette Bradley; would Miss Stevens please call her room.

Felicia slowly put down the phone. She could ignore it, pretend she'd already left the hotel.

She went to the bathroom, cleaned her teeth, and checked that she hadn't left anything behind. Then she lifted the receiver and asked to be put through to Suzette's room.

'Hello?' Suzette's voice was low and slightly breathless.

'It's Felicia. You wanted to speak to me?'

'Oh, yeah.' A short, curious silence ensued as though Suzetfe had put her hand momentarily over the receiver. Felicia had a sudden heartstopping thought. Had Suzette and Joshua spent the night together, consoling each other? Maybe this was his idea, some kind of twisted revenge.

But no, Suzette surely wouldn't have gone along with anything like that.

'Thanks for calling back.' Suzette's voice came on the line again. 'Er... about last night...'

'You don't owe me any explanations,' Felicia cut in. 'Joshua's a free agent.'

'I just thought—are you sure you're not making a big mistake?'

Not as big a mistake as Genevieve did, Felicia thought bleakly. 'Look, it's sweet of you,' she said, 'but as far as I'm concerned there's nothing between me and Joshua. If you weren't going back to Canada...'

'Yeah, what?' Suzette asked curiously.

'I'd be warning you to watch out for yourself,' Felicia answered. 'Not to get tangled up with him.'

'Well...thanks for the thought. I appreciate that.'

Felicia gave a small laugh. 'You're welcome.'

'You know,' Suzette said, her voice dropping to a confidential tone, 'you and I ought to get together for some girl-talk, without any guys.'

Felicia firmly banished from her mind the image of Joshua lounging on the bed next to Suzette. 'I'd have liked that, but I have a plane to catch.'

'Oh, shame! What time?'

Warning bells rang in Felicia's mind. 'I'll be leaving the hotel pretty soon.'

'Oh, well, have a good flight. Listen, if you're ever in Toronto look me up. I'll give you my address and phone number. Got a pen?'

Felicia picked up the hotel notepad by the phone and scribbled down the number, knowing she'd never use it. When Suzette asked, 'What's yours? I've always wanted to visit New Zealand someday,' she could scarcely refuse to reciprocate.

'I'll give you the address of my shop,' she said. 'It's easy to find.'

* * *

Fearing that Joshua might be at the airport, Felicia didn't breathe easily until she boarded the plane. At the end of the long flight she stumbled off at Mangere, got a taxi home, and fell thankfully into her own bed. She had a weekend to get over any jet lag before returning to work alongside her friend and business partner, Shelley Langham.

On Monday morning Shelley, a tall redhead with a swag of curls hitched high to one side and swinging to her shoulders, greeted her with, 'Home is the traveller! How was it?'

'Fascinating. Also hot, hectic, and I need another holiday to get over this one.'

'Mmm, you look a bit hollow-eyed. Been burning the midnight oil over there, have you?'

'Very little, actually. I'll tell you all about it,' Felicia lied, 'and bore you with my holiday snaps.' After she had removed the ones that inevitably included Joshua Tagget, and burned them. 'How's business?'

'Not bad for this time of year. I sold that kauri towel rack at last.'

'You did?' Felicia turned to where the rack had stood near the door when she left. A magnificent but expensive piece fashioned by a local wood-turner, it had proved unexpectedly difficult to sell. 'That's great.' The commission would help their profit margin.

She soon slipped back into the rhythm of her life, the routine of the shop, and the easy if not overly intimate relationships that she had developed with a small circle of good friends.

But she was unable to dispel a sense of emptiness and loss, a revival of emotions she had buried years ago. What she had done in China should have exorcised the last vestiges of pain; instead she found herself reliving it nightly. The dreams had returned to haunt her. And now they contained an added, disturbing element, the old fantasies mingled with new, potent images of a misty Chinese mountainscape and a dark man standing at the foot of a waterfall, staring into a fathomless pool—of him reaching out to her, then sinking with her into the depths. The water would close about them, but she was never afraid. Too often she woke with her body throbbing in remembered need that was never fulfilled.

When one day she looked up from wrapping a pair of pillowcases in gift paper for a customer and saw Joshua standing in the doorway of the shop, she was convinced this was another dream. Calmly she went on sealing the parcel, handing it to the customer with the receipt, saying, 'Thank you, come again.'

Then she put her hands flat on the small counter to steady herself and watched Joshua walk across the floor, his amber eyes holding hers with a stare that was curious but cold.

Shelley had gone out for a late lunch break and Felicia was alone in the shop. Not that there was anything to worry about, supposing this wasn't a nightmare after all. Joshua would hardly be planning to attack her.

He didn't look too friendly though, as he planted his hands on the other side of the counter in mockery of her stance and said quietly, 'Hello, Felicia.'

Oddly, it was the familiar, faint scent of him that convinced her she wasn't going to wake up this time.

In a suit and tie with a striped shirt, he looked big and businesslike, but his eyes held little points of light, and the tiny crease by his mouth deepened momentarily as he regarded her.

'Joshua.' She swallowed, annoyed that her voice had come out breathy and uncertain. 'This is a surprise. What are you doing in Auckland? You're a long way from...Palmerston North, isn't it?'

'You remembered,' he said, smooth satire in his tone. 'I'm attending a conference on the latest computer-related manufacturing techniques for machine parts, among other things.'

'I see.' She didn't, though. She took her hands from the counter, folding her arms in an instinctively protective gesture. 'So...are you looking for a gift to take back for...someone?'

'I was looking for you.'

Any hope that he had walked in accidentally died an abrupt death. 'How...how did you know where to find me?' She had been carefully vague about the whereabouts of the shop, and had never told him its distinctive name—Cleopatra's.

'Suzette,' he said, confirming a suspicion that had haunted her for weeks. So she wasn't being paranoid after all.

'A traitor to her sex,' Felicia said bitterly. 'I might have known she didn't want my address for herself.'

He gave a crack of reluctant laughter. 'I bribed her with a handsome dinner to find it out.'

'I didn't think you'd ever want to see me again.'

His soft voice was like an icy finger down her spine. 'You were wrong.' He straightened suddenly and reached out a hand, loosely clenched, running the back of one knuckle down to the corner of her mouth.

Despite the deliberate lightness of his touch, Felicia flinched.

He dropped his hand, thrusting it into his trouser pocket, so that the edge of his jacket was hooked back.

'When you made it clear you'd led me up the garden path, and had no intention of explaining why, I told myself a woman like that wasn't worth wasting my time and my temper on. I figured you were waiting for me to create some kind of scene, make an even bigger fool of myself, and give you something more to...giggle about. And I wasn't going to give you the satisfaction. I was...bruised and angry, but I thought I'd get over it.'

Felicia couldn't look at him any more. Her eyes fixed on the counter before her, she said, 'Then why have you come to find me?'

He didn't answer for a moment or two. When he did, his voice was low and hard. 'It didn't quite work out like that. I still want you,' he said. 'And I intend to have you—again.'

It sounded like a threat. She lifted her eyes to his, shock and anger stiffening her spine. 'Not if I have anything to say about it!'

He grinned, and if the wolfish gleam hadn't still been in his eyes she'd have thought it a genuine smile. 'I'm sure you'll have a lot to say.'

'I believed I'd made it clear to you—'

'Oh, abundantly. You wouldn't care to tell me why you felt it necessary to be so...clear?'

Maybe she would. He still hadn't worked it out, she guessed. 'All right,' she said recklessly, but was interrupted by someone else entering the shop.

The middle-aged couple browsed for a while, asked questions, and left without buying anything, but by that time two more people had come in. Shelley returned from lunch, and still Joshua was pretending to inspect the shelves of coloured towels, embroidered and frilled bed linen, fragrant soaps and bath salts, and jars of pot-pourri.

Shelley approached him with a smile, and Felicia, occupied with a customer, saw them speak, then Shelley came behind the counter to her side, and Joshua at last left.

'Your friend said he'd be back,' Shelley informed her when the rush of custom was over. 'You didn't tell me about him.' Her look was speculative, teasing. 'You were on the same tour in China, he said.'

'Yes.' Felicia turned away, busying herself with stacking a pile of credit card slips and stowing them in a drawer.

'And he's come looking you up? You don't seem thrilled.'

'Maybe that's because I'm not.'

'Oh.' Shelley looked crestfallen. 'I take it he has a fatal flaw. Pity. He looked very promising.'

'Looks can be deceiving.'

Shelley sighed. 'Don't I know it. What is it—cloth between the ears? Octopus syndrome? Or he's married? He's not a secret axe murderer?'

Reluctantly Felicia smiled a little grimly. 'Not exactly—as far as I know.'

'Then what have you got against him?'

'A lot,' Felicia said succinctly, and then the door opened and another rush began.

He was there again when they were ready to close up for the day, coming inside as Felicia approached the doorway.

'We're closing,' she said. 'Sorry.'

'I know,' Joshua replied. 'Can I take you home?'

'No. I need to lock the door.'

'Don't let me stop you.' He moved to one side and waited.

Felicia gritted her teeth. 'Will you please leave?'

'I want to talk to you.'

'It's not mutual.'

He glanced behind her, to where Shelley was hovering near the counter. 'If we're going to discuss issues of mutuality,' he suggested, 'you might prefer to do that in private.'

'I'm not discussing anything with you.'

A woman walked in through the still-open door, glanced at them and went to the counter. 'You're not closed yet?' she begged Shelley. 'I need a wedding present in a hurry.'

'Look around,' Shelley invited her, and went to shut the door herself. Turning to Felicia, she raised her brows. 'Why don't you take your friend into the back room? I can finish up here.'

Joshua actually smiled at her. 'Thank you.'

Of course Shelley didn't want them standing here glowering and hissing at each other. It was bad for business. And obviously Joshua wasn't going to give in and quietly leave. Felicia silently led him behind the counter, then through the swing door leading to the all-purpose room at the rear where they kept boxes of stock for which there wasn't room on the shop floor, and things like unused display stands and empty cartons. There was also a computer desk, a corner for tea-making, a small microwave oven, and a shabby sofa.

Felicia didn't invite Joshua to sit down. Swinging round to face him, she began, 'I don't know what you think you're going to gain from this—'

'An explanation,' he said evenly, 'would be nice.'

Conscious of the murmur of voices from the shop, she knew that if she raised hers it would be all too audible. Besides, she dared not allow the words to tumble out willy-nilly. She took a deep breath, trying for calm.

Perhaps he misinterpreted her hesitation. 'Did you think I'd just meekly walk away with my tail between my legs?' he demanded, his voice low but savage. 'Maybe you've got away with it before, but this time you've picked the wrong man. I don't take kindly to being made a fool of. So what game were you playing?'

'Do you need to ask? I'd have thought it was one you were very familiar with—only it looks different when you're on the receiving end, doesn't it?' She found that her hands were clenched, and consciously loosened them.

His eyes were piercing, his face alert, thoughtful. 'What have I ever done to you?' he asked. 'Or are you taking revenge for what some other guy did, is that it? A bit unfair, surely?' He took a step towards her, his expression changing, softening a little. 'Some louse hurt you, and you took it out on me?'

'As you said,' Felicia answered, 'that would be unfair.'

The line between his brows deepened. 'That's *not* it? Then what—?' He reached out in frustration, grasping her upper arms.

She felt his touch right through her body, a lick of fire that seared instantly along her veins. Her eyes widened in shock, and she saw his darken with unexpected desire.

No! But even as she thought it, her spine arched slightly, instinctively, her body yearning towards him.

Then he pulled her close, his hands closing tightly on her arms, and his mouth was on hers, hot and open and starving for her.

As she was starving for him. The prickling awareness that his presence invariably aroused in her turned instantly to fierce, sizzling desire, each individual hair lifting from her scalp, every nerve-end like an exposed wire, invisible sparks dancing along her skin.

He made a low sound in his throat and his arms came about her, wrapping her closer. She felt her head fall back under the pressure of his insistent mouth, and fought for will-power, for sanity, for the strength to push him away.

With clenched hands she shoved against his chest, forced her body to rigidity, to resistance, somehow wrenched her mouth away from its seductive captivity. 'Let me go!' she panted. 'Let *go*!'

He loosened his grip and she stumbled back, raising a hand to wipe it across her burning mouth. 'Don't you *touch* me!' she said, furious to find that her voice was shaking and too high. 'Don't you ever touch me again!'

He looked dazed, his face dusky with colour, his mouth clamped in a rigid line. He thrust his hands into his pockets, and she saw his throat move as he swallowed hard. Harshly, he said, 'I don't understand you.'

'What part of *no* don't you understand?'

'The part where you kiss me back!' he shot at her. 'The part where you practically turn to fire in my arms, the part where your body melts so sweetly against mine and begs me to love you.'

'You're imagining—'

'I'm *imagining* nothing!' he interrupted. 'If you found me repulsive I could make some sense of it, but it's obvious that you don't—'

'The voice of experience!' Felicia sneered.

His eyes sharpened, narrowed. 'Some,' he acknowledged. 'Enough to know that however you deny it you want to make love to me. Is it a crime that I'm not inexperienced? Does it bother you?'

'*You* are bothering me! I don't want you; I don't even like you!'

'That's a lie!'

'You must have an elephantine ego!'

He almost grinned. 'No—but I'm not a fool. Are you committed to someone? You said in China there was no one, but you were on holiday—did you decide to have a fling, a bit of an adventure on the side?'

She opened her mouth to deny it, then heard herself say in a strange tone, 'And if I was...committed to someone else, would you walk away, leave me alone?'

His face changed, as though she'd administered a shock, and then he said slowly, his eyes narrowing, 'Maybe not. Maybe I'd take you away from him.'

Her head up, she said, 'You really think you could?'

Softly, taking a step closer to her, he said, 'Is that what you want, Felicia? Does that excite you?'

Excite her? Nausea rose inside her and she had to force it down. 'No,' she said baldly. 'It disgusts me. You disgust me.' In that moment it was very nearly true. How she wished it to be wholly true.

Joshua grinned openly, totally disbelieving. 'Is that so?' he taunted. 'Shall I kiss you again and you can show me again just how much I disgust you?'

Hastily Felicia retreated, until she was stopped by the sofa behind her calves. 'Keep your hands off me!'

'There's nothing to be frightened of, Felicia. I won't touch you again unless you ask.' He sounded almost soothing. But his eyes were dark and intense, deep golden fires smouldering in them.

'Don't hold your breath,' she advised, her bravado more for herself than him.

Joshua laughed quietly. 'I quit doing that when I was a teenager.'

'I wasn't talking about—' She stopped there, realising the trap he'd led her into.

'Never mind,' he said kindly, 'we can discuss kissing techniques another time.'

There was a discreet tapping on the door, and then Shelley pushed it open. 'Everything OK?' she asked tentatively. 'I've closed up in front.'

'Thanks.' Felicia smiled blindly at her. 'Joshua's just leaving.'

'You can go out this way,' Shelley told him helpfully, indicating the rear door.

'Thanks, I'll wait for Felicia.'

Felicia gritted her teeth. Shelley gave her a questioning, anxious look. Felicia reviewed her options and finally said, 'I'll lock up, Shelley. You go.' She didn't want Shelley embroiled in this, and short of calling the police, a gross overreaction that would involve all kinds of embarrassing questions and explanations, she couldn't think of any way of getting rid of him.

Shelley said doubtfully, 'Are you sure? I don't mind waiting.' She glanced at Joshua.

'I'm sure,' Felicia said. 'Joshua and I haven't quite finished talking.'

At that, Shelley evidently deduced quite wrongly that Felicia couldn't wait to be alone with her visitor. She smiled apologetically, gathered up her bag and quickly left.

When the back door had closed behind her, Joshua turned an alert, enquiring look on Felicia.

'So,' he said, 'are you going to tell me who my rival is?'

'Your rival?'

'Loyalty is very admirable, Felicia, but it already slipped a bit in China, didn't it? You're not married to him, are you? Somehow you don't seem married.'

'I'm not married,' Felicia said automatically. Would it have made any difference to him if she had been?

Of course not, she answered herself. He didn't have any respect for marriage vows. To him they were nothing more than a minor inconvenience.

A flicker of relief crossed his face all the same. 'Then,' he said, 'all's fair.'

'You're prepared to wreck any relationship I might have?' she asked him, rage stirring deep inside. 'Even though you know I don't want to have an affair with you?'

'If you really don't want to,' he said, 'you won't. I can't force you into it. So where's the problem?'

The problem, as he had so accurately diagnosed, was in her wholly inappropriate, immature, and ill-advised response to him.

'You're unscrupulous,' she said. 'Unprincipled and unscrupulous. You don't give a damn for anyone's happiness if it gets in the way of your temporary gratification. You're selfish and greedy and... and faithless.'

Joshua was frowning. 'Where did you get these notions? *Faithless?*' he repeated.

Felicia flushed. She supposed the archaic word sounded rather silly. But it was the word she needed. 'I'm not being loyal to any man,' she said. It was time to let him know. 'I'm being loyal to a memory—the memory of my sister.'

'Your sister?' He looked utterly blank.

'Genevieve,' Felicia said, watching his face, waiting while the bafflement turned to swift, appalled comprehension, then stunned disbelief.

'Genevieve,' he said, staring at her as though his gaze would penetrate her skin, strip away the layers of maturity that had overlaid the smooth childish face he scarcely remembered. 'Genevieve,' he repeated, and she saw that she had finally rocked him, and was glad. 'Your sister?' He shook his head, then stared at her again. 'Lissa,' he said slowly. 'Good God! That's why I had that nagging feeling we'd met before. You're Lissa!'

CHAPTER SEVEN

'YES.' It was a relief to acknowledge it at last. 'I'm Lissa.'
No one had called her that for years.

'Lissa,' Joshua repeated softly. 'You've certainly
grown up. Beautifully.' His gaze moved over her like a
caress, and she stiffened. As his eyes met hers again, the
half-smile that had begun to form on his lips abruptly
faded. 'Why didn't you tell me? Why keep it a secret all
this time?'

'It was no secret. I thought . . . I expected you'd recognise my name, at least.'

'Felicia? But I didn't know that was your name. And
I don't believe I ever heard your surname.'

He probably hadn't, she realised. The summer she had
spent the school holidays staying with Genevieve she'd
been a child, introduced as 'my little sister, Lissa'. He
might never have heard her called anything else. No
wonder he hadn't recognised her in Beijing.

He said, 'Were you offended that I didn't remember
you? Is that why . . . ? But you surely wouldn't—' The
frown between his brows deepened. 'I don't understand,' he reiterated slowly. 'What have I ever done to
you?'

He was unbelievable, Felicia thought. He still didn't
have a clue. 'It wasn't what you did to *me*,' she said,
her voice harsh with the effort to keep it steady, not to
scream at him, hurl herself upon him bodily and pummel
him with her fists. 'It's what you did to Genevieve.'

'Genevieve?' His eyes had darkened again, and his lips tightened. 'You were a child,' he said. 'You couldn't possibly have any inkling—'

'I might have been young, but I wasn't as stupid as you think!' Felicia threw at him. 'I was the go-between!'

'I know.' He looked momentarily uncomfortable, a faint line of colour lying on his cheekbones. 'That was...a mistake. It wasn't fair to involve you.'

'I didn't mind. For Genevieve. I'd have done anything for her! But you...how *could* you? You *betrayed* her!'

Shock instantly wiped his face clean of all expression, but she scarcely noticed. Her eyes had filled with hot, swimming tears, humiliating her, and she turned away from him in a desperate, fruitless bid to hide them.

His hand closed on her shoulder, she heard his voice say her name, and she whirled around, wrenching herself out of his light hold. 'I told you, don't *touch* me!' Angrily she dashed a hand across her eyes, but it didn't stop the tears. 'Go away!' she cried wildly. 'Go away and don't ever come near me again!'

'No. What the hell does Genevieve have to do with what happened between us?' he demanded.

'Work it out for yourself!' she advised him, dangerously close to hysteria. 'It shouldn't be that hard!'

He reached a hand towards her, and she swung her arm and hit it away, hurting herself more than him. 'What does it take to get through to you?' she said, gritting her teeth. 'I want you *out of here*! Do I have to call the police?'

'No.' Joshua finally stepped back.

'Go on—go!' Felicia reiterated, choking.

'I can't leave you like this—'

Between her teeth, she said, 'It's *you* that's making me like this! I told you, get out!'

He stared at her, then seemed to make a decision. 'Obviously I'm not going to get through to you right now. I didn't intend to distress you...Lissa. But some time we have to talk. I'll be back.'

He hesitated a moment longer, while she stood before him with tears scalding down her cheeks, too proud to make the futile gesture of trying to wipe them away again. Then he swung on his heel and left, closing the door decisively behind him.

Felicia sank into a huddle in a corner of the ancient sofa and laid her head on her folded arms, weeping as she had not done since Genevieve's death.

'Are you all right?' Shelley asked the following morning. 'You look a bit under the weather.'

'Headache,' Felicia explained truthfully. She had slept but her dreams had been agitated, depressing, and two aspirins had failed to cure the pounding at her temples.

'Late night?' Shelley queried, her curiosity showing in a sidelong glance. 'Did your mystery man entice you to go out with him after all?'

'No.' To soften the denial, Felicia reluctantly added, 'He left soon after you did.'

'I see.' She patently didn't, but Felicia was glad of her friend's sensitivity and discretion. Nothing more was said about Joshua's visit.

That didn't stop Felicia from thinking about him, though. Unfortunately it was a slow day for custom, and that left her far too much time to do so.

Late in the afternoon a florist's van pulled up in the loading zone outside the shop, and the driver descended from it with a large bouquet of white and yellow roses, then pushed open the door. 'Felicia Stevens?'

Shelley indicated Felicia. Guessing who the flowers were from, Felicia reluctantly took them, tempted to throw them straight into the nearest rubbish bin as the driver left the shop, but inhibited from the melodramatic gesture by Shelley's presence.

'They're gorgeous! Lucky girl. Aren't you going to look at the card?' Shelley asked.

Felicia put down the bouquet on the counter as a customer entered the shop. Shelley gave the woman a professional smile. 'Good afternoon, can I help you?' Apparently she could. While she looked for a particular shade of matching bath accessories, Felicia found the small envelope pinned to the Cellophane, with the inscription *Lissa,* and after a moment's hesitation lifted the seal.

I'm sorry if I upset you, she read. *Returning to Palmerston North today. Will be in touch.* And the slashing signature.

She gave herself the meagre satisfaction of tearing the note up with quick, vicious movements, then carried the flowers out to the back room and dumped them in the sink.

'You can have them,' she told Shelley indifferently later. 'I can't be bothered taking them on the bus.' Although she owned a car, most days she used public transport. Her flat, part of a converted old house in Mount Eden, was only a ten-minute journey from the city centre.

'They'd look good in the shop,' Shelley suggested, 'unless having them there would bother you...?'

'Of course it wouldn't bother me,' Felicia said too hastily. 'Put them in the shop if you like.'

Shelley arranged them in a tall white china ewer and placed them on the antique washstand that served as a display unit for bathroom linen and toiletries. Over the next few days their subtle perfume coloured the air. Felicia wished she had insisted on Shelley taking them home. When the petals turned limp and began falling, she took the ewer out the back and dropped the flowers unceremoniously into the plastic rubbish container under the sink.

Returning to the shop, she trod on one of a trail of petals scattered over the floor, releasing the sweet, spicy perfume.

Bending, she scooped up the bruised, fragrant scraps and got rid of them before serving the next customer.

But when she went home the scent of roses still clung to her.

The following day she turned from the washstand where she was rearranging a display of a new brand of oils and essences that had been depleted by the last customer, and found Joshua looming in the doorway.

There were several people in the shop, and Shelley was showing one of them the latest range of duvet covers. Joshua glanced about him and went straight to Felicia's side.

With shaking fingers she unnecessarily moved a blue glass flagon of perfumed oil a few inches to one side. 'Why are you here? I told you not to—'

'We have some unfinished business to attend to.'

'No.' Presenting her back to him, she placed a matching blue jar of cotton wool balls alongside the flagon.

It was a mistake. She felt the warmth of him behind her as his hands clamped down on the washstand, trapping her between his arms. *'Yes,'* he said in her ear. His voice was kept low, but every word was distinct. 'We can discuss it here and now if you like, or privately later. Your choice.' He glanced at the placard on the door that stipulated the shop's opening hours. 'You have to stay late tonight?' They didn't close on Fridays until eight-thirty.

Felicia trembled, her spine tingling as she strained to avoid any physical contact with him.

'I could come back at half past eight,' he said.

She cast a desperate, hunted glance to one side, but everyone seemed oblivious to her predicament, Shelley holding up another mat for a customer's inspection, while several others talked quietly to each other, turning over stock to find the price tags.

'Lissa?' His breath stirred a strand of hair against the sensitive skin below her ear when he murmured the name.

'All right,' she capitulated. As soon as he removed his hands she spun round to face him, her cheeks flushed with anger. 'But it's the last time.'

'We'll see.' He hadn't moved far—not at all in fact, except for his hands, now thrust into his pockets. He was still much too close, regarding her with a strange, enigmatic expression. 'Thank you.'

Then he nodded at her, wheeled about and left the shop. Shelley hadn't even noticed he was there, Felicia guessed. Yet she felt as if she'd been touched by a whirlwind.

Somehow she got through the rest of the afternoon. Shelley left at five, because she and her husband were attending the performance of a new opera tonight, with dinner first. Friday nights were usually not too busy, and Felicia had been confident of holding the fort on her own. She was relieved that Shelley wouldn't be around when Joshua appeared again.

He arrived as she was closing the doors. Her last customer had left ten minutes before, and Felicia had started cashing up early, tempted to shut up shop and slip out the back way before he came, but that would be cowardly, and only postpone the inevitable.

He strode into the shop and allowed her to shoot the bolts home behind him.

'All right,' she said, facing him defiantly. He was wearing casual dun slacks and a cream shirt without a tie, the collar open and the sleeves rolled to the elbows. 'Say what you want to say, and then go.'

He regarded her thoughtfully. 'Not standing around here. This'll take a bit longer than five minutes.' He looked about the showroom, his gaze lingering briefly on the antique brass bed made up with a pristine white crochet cover, and the array of jewel-coloured satin-embossed towels that hung on the foot rail. 'Have you eaten?' he asked.

She'd had a snack at around five-thirty. Usually she would have gone home and made herself a toasted sandwich or an omelette. 'I'm not hungry,' she told him.

'I suggest we go back to my hotel,' Joshua said. 'And you needn't look like a Sabine sighting the Romans riding over the hills,' he added with a touch of weary cynicism as she lifted her chin, preparing to refuse. 'I'm talking about a drink or two in a quiet corner of the public lounge, followed by supper. Unless you'd like to invite me back to your place? No, I thought not.' He correctly read her expression. 'I suppose if I tell you I already know where you live it won't make any difference?'

It was a shock to her. There were half a dozen F. Stevens entries in the telephone book. If he'd been determined enough, she supposed it wouldn't have taken long to sort out which was hers. It was a wonder he hadn't already contacted her there.

As if he'd read her mind, Joshua said, 'I was tempted to phone you at home.'

'Why didn't you?'

'That's... a bit complicated.'

Someone tapped on the door and he turned. A middle-aged woman holding an armful of parcels stood there with a pleading expression.

'Sorry,' he called through the door, 'the shop's closed. Come back tomorrow.'

Turning his back on the woman's disappointed face, he took Felicia's arm and steered her firmly towards the back of the showroom.

'Since when,' she demanded furiously, 'did you take it on yourself to turn away custom from *my* shop?'

'Since now,' he answered shortly, pushing open the door and thrusting her through it. 'It's after hours.'

Felicia pulled away and rounded on him as the door swung to behind them. 'I don't know how you run *your* business, but here we believe in customer service.'

'I'm sure you'd stay open until midnight if you thought it would postpone having to talk to me! That's what this is really about, isn't it?'

'What it's really about is your taking the decision out of my hands over something that's none of your damned business.'

'All right,' Joshua conceded testily. 'I apologise—OK? Do you want me to run after her and call her back?'

Felicia snapped, 'No, of course not. It's too late now.'

'Good,' he said, raising her hackles again. 'So can we leave now?'

'I haven't finished cashing up.'

'Do it, then.' He was rather obviously holding onto his temper. 'How long will that take?'

'Thank you,' she said sarcastically. 'About fifteen minutes.'

'Can I help?'

'No—thanks. If you want a cup of tea or something, help yourself.' It wasn't a particularly gracious offer, but at least she had mustered some semblance of civility.

When she had finished she found him sitting on the sofa, his long legs stretched out before him, his arms folded as he contemplated, apparently, the toes of his shoes. He stood up, and watched while she put away the day's takings in the small floor safe and collected her bag and a light jacket.

He led her to a rental car parked just around the corner. Trust Joshua, she thought acidly, to be able to find a legal parking space where they were at a premium.

They didn't speak on the short journey to his hotel. He drove into the car park and then led her inside, crossing a wide, marble-floored lobby to a large bar where the hum of conversation and the clink of glasses were muted by thick carpet.

He found them a circular, glass-topped table in a corner, flanked by two tub chairs and half screened with a potted palm. 'I'll get our drinks at the counter,' he said. 'Quicker than waiting for service. What would you like?'

She asked for Irish cream on ice, and watched him stride over to the bar, not missing the interested glances of a couple of women drinking together at a nearby table. One of them said something to the other and they both laughed.

He was back within a minute, placing a glass before Felicia and sitting down with his own in his hand. Somehow he'd also managed to carry a bowl of mixed nuts.

Felicia restrained her admiration for the feat. 'Do you often stay here?' she asked him. It wasn't the most expensive hotel in town, but it had a certain class that didn't come cheap.

'Mostly, when I'm in Auckland,' he said. 'I get a special rate as a regular customer, and it's a good place to deal with clients and contacts, particularly from overseas. There's a very efficient business centre here.'

'Do you have many overseas clients?'

'Several, and I'm always looking for more.'

Felicia picked up her drink and absently swirled the pale brown liquid, the ice cubes making a small tinkling sound against the glass.

'I didn't expect you in Auckland again so soon.'

'I'd have warned you, only I was afraid you might decide to fly the coop.'

She would have too if it hadn't meant letting Shelley down. He was a cunning devil. 'When do you go back to Palmerston North?'

'That depends.'

She risked a look at him. 'On what? Some deal you're negotiating?'

'You could say that.' He had a brandy balloon in his hand, and he tasted the amber liquid. 'I didn't bring you here to talk about my business plans.'

Nervously, Felicia raised her own glass to her lips and sipped at the deceptively creamy mixture, grateful for the underlying bite.

'Why did you say I betrayed Genevieve?' he asked her.

'Because it's true.'

'Lissa, it wasn't like that! Believe me—'

'Why should I? I might have been only a kid but I know what happened. I saw it.'

It seemed a long time before he said anything. Despising herself for not being able to meet his eyes, she watched his long, strong fingers that cupped the brandy balloon as he gently swirled the contents. Then he put the glass decisively down on the table. 'How old were you—twelve?'

'Thirteen.'

He nodded. 'And you had just lost both your parents.'

'Six months before.'

'It must have been traumatic.'

She didn't bother to acknowledge the obvious. 'Your sympathy is appreciated.' But—and he could read it in her tone easily enough—it wasn't going to soften her in any way.

'You were very fond of Genevieve.'

'Yes.' Genevieve had been the one constant, shining star in a black universe after Genevieve's father and Felicia's mother had died in a boating accident. They had both been keen sailors, and if Felicia hadn't been on a school camp that weekend she'd probably have been with them when their runabout overturned coming back from a fishing trip on the Manukau Harbour. Their bodies were washed ashore the following day.

Genevieve and Felicia's one aunt, her mother's sister, had agreed that the best thing for Felicia was a good boarding school, and fortunately her parents' estate provided enough money for that. Alternate school holidays would be spent with Aunt Marise, who had a high-powered government job in Wellington, and Genevieve.

'You can't have been that close,' Joshua said carefully, 'with a nine-year age difference.'

'Twelve,' Felicia corrected him automatically, scarcely registering the fleeting surprise that crossed his hard features. 'Age has nothing to do with it. She was all I had...and vice versa.' Genevieve had said so, more than once.

'Genevieve had a husband,' Joshua reminded her bluntly.

'Oh, you remember that...now?'

He looked at her with a strange, brooding expression. 'Believe me, I never forgot it.'

Believe him? Her lip curled. 'Really?' she mocked him.

'Really.' His voice was harsh, and he suddenly leaned forward, pushing the balloon glass aside. 'All this has some connection, I take it, with what happened in Guangzhou?'

'Top marks for deduction.'

Joshua shook his head. 'I've been over it all in my mind hundreds of times, and I still can't make any sense of it. First you pretend not to know me, then you spend nearly three weeks stringing me along, culminating in...in one night that I'll remember as long as I live—'

She couldn't help the fleeting, upward flick of her eyelids, the quick flash of her eyes, and it stopped him for a full second.

'Then,' he said slowly, 'you deliver the *coup de grâce* in as public a way as possible, calculated to cause me maximum pain and embarrassment, and finally do your best to vanish from my life.'

Only that last part hadn't worked. He'd found her, and now he was demanding answers of her—answers and what else?

His eyes still intent on her face, he went on, 'If I'm being punished for something, at least I'm entitled to know what the crime is. Why did you do it, Lissa? What the hell were you playing at in Guangzhou?'

CHAPTER EIGHT

'YOU caused Genevieve's death!' Felicia said. 'And you wonder why I wanted to hurt you a little?'

'A little?' His face was taut and angry, his eyes ablaze. She saw him take control with a visible effort, and the fist he had clenched on the table slowly uncurled. He looked down at the table-top as if for inspiration, and when his eyes returned to hers his expression was calm, although his face had paled. 'I wasn't responsible for Genevieve's death,' he said flatly. 'You've got it all wrong, Lissa.'

'Oh, not in the sense that you took a gun or knife and deliberately murdered her, but if it wasn't for you she would never have driven her car into that bridge.'

His eyes blanked with shock. '*Suicide?* Lissa—'

'Stop calling me that! My name is Felicia!'

'Sorry,' he said curtly. 'It's just that ever since I found out who you were...are, somehow I've thought of you as Lissa. It seems more...real.'

Real. Felicia blinked. A strange feeling of terror assailed her. Sometimes she experienced momentarily a disorienting sensation that the person called Felicia Stevens didn't exist in an actual sense. That the cool, capable, pleasantly bland young woman who inhabited her body was an impostor, no relation to the impetuous, impassioned, loving child, Lissa.

Under his eyes she had an illogical conviction that he could see through the transparent nothingness that was

Felicia to the frightened, abandoned little girl who lived deep down inside that outer shell.

He must have noticed something in her face. A quick frown appeared between his brows. 'What is it?' he asked. 'What's the matter—Felicia?'

'I just can't stand sitting here with you.'

A muscle twitched just under his eye, but apart from that his expression remained unchanged. 'That's too bad,' he said, 'because I don't intend to let you go until we've straightened this out between us.'

He might as well have waved a red rag. Felicia grabbed at her bag and put a hand on the table to give her leverage to push back the chair.

Joshua leaned forward again, his hand clamping hers against the polished wood edge of the table-top. With his eyes down, he said in a low voice, 'I mean it. If you want to leave you'll need to scream the place down and get them to call the cops, because one way or another I'm going to get to the bottom of this thing.' He raised his eyes at last, and she looked into their implacable depths and knew he wasn't bluffing.

She glared right back at him, conscious of his heavy grip cutting off the circulation in her wrist. Their eyes duelled for long seconds, neither of them prepared to give in.

Finally she said, 'Five minutes.'

He inclined his head and sat back slowly, gradually releasing the pressure on her hand, his fingers sliding over her skin like a caress before they left her completely.

Felicia glanced pointedly at her watch.

He picked up the glass and downed the remainder of his brandy in one swallow. 'All right,' he said. 'Let's start with why you imagine I somehow caused Genevieve to kill herself.'

She hadn't expected him to return the ball to her court. Was he deliberately twisting the knife, making her put into words what they both knew perfectly well?

'She thought you loved her,' she accused him. 'She was ready to give up everything for you and then you let her down. You were leading her on when all the time you didn't mean any of it.'

His eyes narrowed, and she saw his jaw tauten as if holding back a retort. 'Actually it was the other way round.'

Her eyes widened in disbelief. What was he saying? 'You told her you loved her!'

Joshua gave a curt, reluctant nod. 'At the time I thought I did. Felicia, you have to understand—'

'I understand perfectly, thank you. Genevieve was in love with you and you deserted her when she expected you to follow through on your promises—when she became a . . . an inconvenience.' As he opened his mouth in protest, she said swiftly, viciously, 'Don't try to deny it. I saw you tear up her last letter to you—without even bothering to read it!'

Very quietly he said, 'So you think I dumped Genevieve. And when we met in China you decided to do the same thing to me?'

'I thought it would do you good to find out what it was like to be on the receiving end for once.'

'Revenge,' he said. 'With interest.'

'You got off lightly.'

'You think so?' His voice grated.

'I don't see *you* climbing into a car and running it into a bridge abutment.'

'You really believe Genevieve did that?' He raised his brows in disbelief. 'Look, I know you were fond of your sister—stepsister, but...' he paused '...at thirteen I don't suppose you were capable of recognising how shallow her emotions really were.'

For a moment anger, red and raw, stopped her breath and speech entirely. As he began to speak again she cut across him, her voice kept low by virtue of a supreme effort of will but shaking badly. '*Her* emotions were shallow? How can *you* say that about Genevieve?'

'Maybe because it's true.'

'It is *not* true! You *bastard*!' she blazed at him. 'You think because she's dead you can slander her name and get away with it—'

'For God's sake, Lissa, you were a child at the time! What could you possibly have known about adult emotions? You don't have any idea what was really going on—'

'I knew exactly what was going on—except that I thought you cared about her! We were both wrong about that—Genevieve and I.'

'What did she tell you?' Joshua asked. He looked slightly shocked. 'Surely she realised you were too young to be her confidante.'

'She didn't think so.' That had daunted him, she saw. He had thought no one knew what was between him and Genevieve. 'I was young, yes. But she trusted me, and who else did she have?'

'So she gave you her version of events, and you swallowed it whole.'

'Are you implying that Genevieve lied to me?' Even though she tried to keep it down, her voice rang with challenge. Her cheeks burned. 'My God, you'll sink to any depths, won't you? She isn't here to defend herself, so you can say whatever you like!'

'I'm not trying to blacken her name, only—'

'You couldn't!' Felicia told him unequivocally. 'Not to me! She was the sweetest, kindest, most generous, *trusting* person I've ever known—or will ever know! And what you did to her was despicable—'

Joshua broke in. 'I'm not proud of it, but believe me, I didn't cause—'

'Why the hell *should* I believe you—you liar!'

'Just what grounds,' he bit out the words, 'do you have for saying that?'

'I was there!' She leaned forward across the table to emphasise her point. 'Remember? I wasn't so young that I was unaware that you and Genevieve were lovers.'

His breath hissed in. 'Did she tell you that? A thirteen-year-old?'

'She didn't need to tell me—I would have guessed anyway. And I saw you once—' Remembering that, she stopped short, flushing.

'Saw me? Saw...us?' His eyes hardened.

'In the sandhills,' she said. 'I wasn't spying, but you weren't always very discreet, were you?'

There was a long pause. He didn't take his steady gaze off Felicia's face and his expression hardly altered, but there was a subtle change. His eyes darkened, and she saw the muscles of his throat contract as he swallowed. 'No,' he said at last. 'Not always.' His chest heaved on a sudden breath. 'For a short time we were lovers.'

It had been a short time—one summer that had changed her life profoundly, and led to Genevieve ending hers, yet Joshua seemed hardly touched by it. He had walked away without a backward glance when everyone else was shattered. Even Paul had been clearly grief-stricken at his young wife's funeral, his normally straight shoulders bowed, his face beneath the stylishly trimmed greying hair hollowed and for once reflecting his true age.

Joshua hadn't even turned up.

'The thing is,' he said now in rather careful tones, 'it wasn't the big deal you seem to think it was.'

She was so angry that her stomach made a nauseated revolution. 'Not for you, obviously!'

'Actually, I was talking about Genevieve.'

'Oh, that's right—her emotions were so shallow that she wasn't capable of any real feeling.'

'I didn't say—'

'You certainly implied it.'

Joshua drew in a breath, seemed about to say something, and then halted. The slight frown between his brows deepened as he hesitated. 'I'm sorry if... if my picture of her doesn't fit with the memories you cherish so much.'

'Your picture of her—the picture you're so intent on giving me—doesn't fit the facts. Do you seriously expect me to believe that Genevieve broke her marriage vows for a meaningless fling? That she wasn't genuinely in love with you?'

'The only genuine thing about her—' He stopped there abruptly, his eyes scanning her flushed, furious face. 'No, forget I said that.'

Felicia couldn't, of course. But she sat tight-lipped and waited for him to go on.

'Do you think I persuaded her to break her vows?' he asked. 'It wasn't quite like that.' Shaking his head, he added as if feeling his way, 'To you she must have seemed

an angel in disguise. You'd have been missing your
mother, a lonely, sad child looking for someone to love
and look up to. It's natural you'd endow your stepsister
with all the virtues. She looked the part too, I'll grant
you. A real golden girl. Pretty and affectionate and full
of laughter—in lots of ways I suppose she was good for
you—'

'She was *wonderful*!' Felicia couldn't help inter-
rupting. He had brought back a vivid memory of
Genevieve, gold-blonde hair that had never seen a dye-
bottle curling gently around a face that was perfectly
oval, with clear blue eyes and a soft, ultra-feminine
mouth that she liked to paint poppy-red. And that smile,
always ready to break into laughter. Except when heartbreak intervened, bringing a tremble to the luscious lips
and veiling her eyes with tears. Unexpectedly, just
thinking about the brutal destruction of that loveliness
in a mangled car, Felicia felt tears prickling in her own
eyes.

'Nobody's perfect, Liss—Felicia,' Joshua said, a new
gentleness in his tone.

'I know that! Her problem was that she was such a
loving person. If she'd been less generous, less giving of
herself—'

A very strange expression crossed his face. For a
second or two he appeared totally at a loss. 'Maybe
you're right,' he said noncommittally. 'Do you mean you
know about her... propensities?'

'Propensities?' Felicia stared at him. 'What the hell
is that supposed to mean?'

Momentarily he pursed his lips, looking rather rueful.
'Never mind. I was... just thinking aloud.'

'No, you weren't. You asked me a question. What does it *mean*? I can't answer if I don't know what you're even talking about, can I?'

'It doesn't matter. You've answered it anyway.'

'I have?' By not understanding it? 'Will you please explain?'

He seemed to be debating it, but finally he shook his head decisively. 'No. It wouldn't do any good, and . . . in any case, you wouldn't believe me.'

'That seems likely,' she said, and looked at her watch again. 'You've had your five minutes.' She saw no point in prolonging this. 'Thank you for the drink.' She got to her feet, hardly having touched the Irish cream.

'Wait.' Joshua rose too. 'I hoped . . . I've booked a table for us in the restaurant.'

'Without asking me? Sorry, but you'll just have to unbook it. I have things to do.'

He followed her as she threaded her way through the tables, moving as swiftly as she could. The bar was very crowded now, some people having shifted chairs to accommodate extra numbers in their groups, and her progress was impeded. Joshua didn't touch her again but she was very conscious of his silent presence right behind her until they reached the lobby.

'I'll get you a cab,' he offered.

'I'll take a bus, thanks.'

'Felicia—please. Let me get you a cab. I'll pay.'

She turned, ready to refuse again, but the thought of walking to a bus stop and waiting in the dark didn't appeal. 'Get one, then,' she said, 'and *I'll* pay.'

He wanted to argue, she saw, but he controlled his exasperation and gave her a tight nod, then pushed through the doors and stepped onto the carriageway.

Within thirty seconds he was holding open the door of a taxi for her, giving the driver her address.

He'd memorised it, she thought with a slight chill as the vehicle drew away from the hotel. He hadn't been bluffing when he said he knew where she lived.

She half expected Joshua to turn up again at the shop on Saturday morning, and was relieved when they closed the doors at twelve with no sign of him. Shelley had been regaling her with a description of the opera in between serving customers, and didn't seem to notice Felicia's state of nervous tension.

Saturday afternoon was when Felicia cleaned the flat. She had just filled the washing machine and was vacuuming the carpet when the telephone rang and she picked it up, switching off the cleaner with her foot.

'Felicia,' Joshua's quiet, deep voice said as the whine of the motor died.

Tempted to hang up in his ear, she quelled the childish impulse and said merely, 'Yes.'

'Are you all right?'

Startled at the question, she replied, 'Shouldn't I be?'

'I thought...you were a bit distressed last night.'

'If I was, do you think hearing from you is going to improve matters?'

'Maybe not.' His voice sounded clipped, fed up. 'But I needed to know.'

'Your concern is noted.'

Astonishingly, he laughed. 'You sound like a politician.'

His laughter, so warm and intimate, brought his face vividly to mind, and she could almost see the small crease curving by his mouth, the glimmer of humour in his eyes. Her hand clenched about the receiver.

'When can I see you again?' he asked suddenly. And added, 'Don't hang up.'

How had he known she was going to? Felicia hesitated. 'I thought the message would have got through to you by now. I don't want—'

'I refuse to believe,' he said, a note of urgency in his voice, 'that you were play-acting the whole time in China. No one is that good an actress.'

'You have no idea how good I am. Or is it just that you can't stand the thought that you finally got beaten at your own game?'

There was a short silence as though he was thinking. Then he said, 'You really enjoyed that, didn't you?'

She hadn't enjoyed it at all. She'd felt sick and horrified and guilty after Guangzhou, and the feelings had never entirely left her, despite her belief that he deserved everything he'd got and much, much more. But she said, *'Yes,'* with as much conviction as she could muster.

Surprisingly he laughed again, a low, vibrant sound. 'Hate me, do you?'

'Yes,' she said again.

'And you haven't got it out of your system yet.'

'What?'

'You're still seething with frustrated anger, it's eating away at you. You'd really like to punish me some more, wouldn't you?'

'What I'd like to do to you,' Felicia said, 'is against the law.'

'You'd let that stop you?'

'I don't see the point in spending ten years in jail on account of a rotten creep like you.'

'Supposing I give you the chance?'

To kill him? Her whole being recoiled. But of course he couldn't mean that. 'What are you talking about?'

'You can't do much to hurt me if we never see each other. I'm offering myself as your whipping boy, since that seems to be what you want.'

The outrageous suggestion took her breath away. 'That's a totally tasteless joke,' she said coldly.

'I'm deadly serious.'

'Then you're mad.'

'Very possibly. I'm not saying I'll take everything you dish out lying down, but I can promise there'll be no physical retaliation.'

'What exactly *are* you saying?' She despised herself for even asking, but curiosity and a peculiar emotion compounded of excitement and trepidation got the better of her.

'Let me take you out to dinner tonight and we'll discuss it.'

'Discuss *what*?'

'Our relationship.'

'We don't have a relationship!'

'Yes, we do, whether you like it or not. Way back to when you were a fey little girl and I was a callow romantic.'

Fey. Was that how she had seemed to him? At thirteen she had been thin and gangly, with long, flyaway hair and an excruciating self-consciousness about the over-prominent front teeth that she tried to hide by seldom breaking into a smile.

Joshua, on the other hand, had been fully adult and the embodiment of teenage fantasy. Assured, handsome, utterly male, and with a smile to die for. She didn't be-

lieve there had ever been anything 'callow' about him.
And as for 'romantic'—that was a laughable euphemism.
'I don't want to talk about that time,' she said.

'Fine, then we won't,' he agreed easily. 'We can talk
about China instead. Have you heard from any of the
tour group?'

'I had a letter from Maggie.' The switch of topic threw
her off-balance. 'She's thinking of holidaying in New
Zealand next year.' This was crazy, indulging in small
talk with Joshua Tagget.

'Uh-huh. I liked Maggie. A woman of sense, I
thought.'

A woman who had thought that Felicia might be
making a grave mistake in dropping Joshua as she had.
Could Maggie have said something to Joshua? Felicia
wondered suspiciously.

'You can tell me more over dinner,' he suggested.

'I haven't agreed—'

'Do,' he interrupted. 'Please...Felicia.'

Felicia knew it had been on the tip of his tongue to
call her Lissa. He was respecting her wishes, and it was
totally illogical to feel a distant sadness at the formality
of his using her full name.

She was hesitating, and he took the chance to press
the point. 'Look on it as a small part of the reparation
you're so determined to extract for my
past...transgressions. You can order the most expensive items on the menu and I'll pay up without a
murmur.'

He could afford it. His company was obviously very
successful. 'Is that a promise?' she asked, recalling that
he'd bribed Suzette with a very expensive dinner in Hong
Kong. He wouldn't find *her* so easy to influence.

'I'll pick you up at seven,' he said. 'We'll go to the best restaurant in town.'

She should have said, I haven't said yes—I won't go. Instead she stayed silently chewing on her lower lip until the phone clicked gently in her ear.

Even as she showered, washed her hair and dried it to a silky sheen, put on a floating, sexy lilac chiffon dress with a low neckline, and slid her feet into grape-coloured high-heeled shoes, she was calling herself all kinds of idiot, rehearsing the words with which she should send Joshua packing. Applying a pink-toned lipstick, she saw that her cheeks were delicately flushed with rose, needing no blusher, the blue of her eyes more intense than usual. She smoothed on a smidgen of eye-shadow, and picked up a mascara wand to touch the tips of her lashes. Her hand was shaking, and she cursed silently and pulled a tissue from the box on her dressing table to remove a blue-black smudge from her cheekbone.

Damn Joshua. He was the only man she'd ever known who could reduce her nerves to this state.

She was ready when he rang the doorbell, but she waited for a second ring before going to answer it, using the time to take several deep, calming breaths, compose her features into a mask of indifference, and without haste gather up her small evening bag and check its contents.

When she finally opened the door Joshua was leaning with one hand on the jamb, looking big and sleek and impatient in a dark suit and tie with a white shirt.

'Sorry to keep you waiting,' she said perfunctorily.

'I doubt it,' he replied. 'But at the risk of sounding hackneyed, it was worth the wait.'

He hadn't moved, and she couldn't pass him where he blocked the doorway. His inspection was thorough and leisurely, raising conflicting emotions compounded of resentment at the frank male scrutiny, and a wholly primitive desire to preen in the light of his evident admiration. She looked good and she knew it, but the confirmation was an added fillip.

At last he straightened and stepped back. 'Shall we go?'

She closed the door and walked past him, her skirt brushing his trouser legs. As she caught a whiff of soap or perhaps aftershave mingled with the faint smell of expensive suiting, she hoped he in turn was tantalised by the fresh, slightly spicy scent arising from her skin where she had touched perfume to her pulse points.

He let her into the car and went round to slide into the driver's seat, finding her fumbling with the seat belt. To her acute annoyance her fingers seemed useless, her hands trembling.

'Here.' He leaned over and fastened it for her. Even though he wasn't touching her, she felt surrounded by the powerful male aura about him. Instinctively her spine pressed against the back of her seat.

He gave her a searching glance but said nothing as he fastened his own seat belt and started the car.

Felicia didn't ask where they were going, but ten minutes later they drew up outside a luxury high-rise hotel, and while a uniformed young man parked the car they were ushered inside.

The restaurant was on one of the upper floors, looking down on the city that curved about the shores of the Waitemata Harbour. Joshua had secured them a window table, and Felicia was glad of the excuse to avoid his eyes on the pretext of admiring the lights studding the streets below, and the tranquil harbour water rapidly dimming from blue to pewter-grey to silky black as night fell over the city.

She didn't order the most expensive dish on the menu, but neither did she stint her choice. True to his word, Joshua never blinked an eyelid. The wine he asked for wasn't a cheap variety either, Felicia noticed. This time she had left the choice entirely to him.

She also left it to him to initiate topics of conversation while they waited for their appetisers, and then for the main course, keeping her replies polite, cool and impersonal. No one could have accused her of rudeness—in fact her manner bordered on over-courteous.

Joshua gave her a couple of long, considering looks, and eventually turned his attention to the grilled hapuka steak in lemon fennel sauce that the waiter set before him.

Relieved, Felicia picked up a fork and attacked the scallops on her plate, poached in white wine and served with buttered baby potatoes and a dish of steamed fresh vegetables. She had thought she was too much on edge to be hungry, but the expertly cooked and deliciously sweet scallops awakened her appetite.

At least eating gave her a good reason not to talk. But when their plates were taken away and the waiter had refilled their wineglasses Joshua made another effort at conversation. 'Remember the first meal we had together, in Beijing? I looked for Huadong vintages on the wine list tonight, but they don't seem to be available here.'

'I never told you,' she said, 'I didn't intend to eat with you at all that evening. It was coincidence that I arrived at the right time.'

Joshua inclined his head, his mouth twisting wryly. 'I see. It wasn't coincidence that I found you walking along the waterfront in Qingdao. I followed you from the hotel.'

'Followed me?'

'You didn't guess? Don't you know that I'd follow you to the ends of the earth and the very gates of hell if necessary?'

It wasn't so much the extravagant statement but the stark note in his voice that widened her eyes and stopped her heart. 'Why?'

He looked at her for a long moment, then slowly shook his head. 'No,' he said. 'You don't hear the words from me again... not until you're ready to return them. Even for you, *Felicia,* I don't grovel.'

She tried to imagine him doing so, and failed. 'You'll never hear them from me,' she warned him. 'Never.'

Even as she said it, the appalling truth burst like an overblown, shimmering bubble in her mind. She might deny him forever, might never let the overused, abused, yet life-transforming phrase 'I love you' pass her lips.

But Joshua wasn't the only one hoist with his own petard.

CHAPTER NINE

'SWEET?' Joshua enquired.

Blinking at what she took for a sudden endearment, Felicia said, 'What?' Had he read her that easily?

'I'm asking if you want a sweet,' Joshua said patiently. He looked at her with some curiosity. 'What's the matter?'

'Nothing.' The waiter approached with the menus and she said, 'Let's have a look, anyway,' glad to hide her face behind the large open pages.

The list of desserts, when she finally focused her mind on them, seemed uniformly rich and sickly. When Joshua said, 'I'd settle for cheese and crackers, myself,' she quickly closed the menu.

'Me too.'

'You're not making the most of your opportunities,' he chided her. 'The chef's specialty would lighten my pocket considerably, even if you didn't eat it.'

'I don't believe in waste.' Or in petty vindictiveness. Making him pay for food she didn't want hardly rated as retribution.

While they waited for the cheese board Joshua asked, 'What happened to you after...after that summer, anyway? In China you shied away from talking about your past. Of course now I understand why.'

'I went back to boarding school,' she said. 'And from then on all my holidays were spent with my aunt Marise in Wellington.'

'How did you get on with her?'

'All right. She couldn't spend much time with me, because of her job. She works at the Beehive.'

'Parliament House? She didn't leave you on your own, surely?'

Felicia shook her head. 'She took some weeks off each year and we'd visit art galleries and museums and have lunch at expensive restaurants. The rest of the time she hired people to keep an eye on me until I was fifteen, and then she said I was old enough to fend for myself. She told me to invite a friend to stay if I liked, but I had the feeling that one teenager was enough for her to cope with. I spent a lot of my time reading or watching TV because I didn't know anyone in Wellington.'

'You must have been lonely.'

Felicia shrugged. 'At school I had friends. And eventually I met . . . people.'

'Boys?'

He was quick. 'Yes, boys. Young men.' Starved for affection, for closeness, she had been foolishly eager to believe herself in love, and learned the hard way that sex and love weren't necessarily synonymous.

Marise, ever practical, had lectured her on safety measures and delivered brisk, impersonal advice, but had neglected to mention the emotional risks of spuriously close physical relationships. That was something that Felicia had eventually worked out for herself. From then on her contact with the opposite sex had been limited to friendship and the occasional exploratory flirtation that had come to nothing. Either the men had become impatient with her reluctance to allow them sexual intimacy, or she had despaired of their commitment to any other kind, and the budding relationships had invariably foundered.

Until Joshua appeared again in her life. And she had made the biggest, costliest mistake she could have ever imagined.

'You were telling the truth when you said there was no one in your life now, though?' Joshua asked her.

'Yes.' There was no reason to lie. 'If there had been I wouldn't have...'

'Slept with me? No, you have a strong sense of loyalty, don't you?'

More than he would ever have, she reminded herself. If he'd any sense of loyalty he would never have done what he had to Genevieve. 'You said we weren't going to talk about that,' she said hastily.

'I said we'd talk about China.'

'I thought you meant—'

'Pagodas and paddy fields? No—how about we discuss the way you snuggled into my body when I put my arms around you, and opened your lips for me so eagerly when I kissed you? Or the teasing way you flicked the tip of your tongue in and out of my mouth when you were aroused, or the way you made me feel when you ran your hands down my chest and over my belly and down to—'

'*Shut up!*' Her face afire, her eyes on the white starched cloth between them, Felicia clutched at the edge of the table-top. 'Stop it or I'll walk out right now.'

It wasn't the best moment for the waiter to deliver the board with its selection of cheeses, garnished with bunches of purple and green grapes on the side.

As he named the half-dozen varieties of cheese for them she was tempted to tip the whole tastefully pre-

sented display over onto the floor and carry out her threat
to leave. But a natural reluctance to create a scene in
public intervened, and she remained sitting stiffly in her
chair after the waiter had left them alone again.

Perhaps Joshua knew he had overstepped the bounds.
'What would you like?' he asked her. 'Kapiti, Gouda,
Brie?'

'I don't care.' Still shaken by the erotic pictures that
had flared into her mind at his low-voiced recollections,
she discovered that her fingers were clamped hard on
the edge of the table-top. Releasing it, she dropped her
hands into her lap. 'I'm not hungry any more.'

Joshua spread some Brie on a cracker and held it out
to her. 'Sure?'

Stubbornly she shook her head. He shrugged and bit
into the cracker himself. After washing it down with a
mouthful of wine, he asked, 'And when you'd left
school, what then?'

'I lived with Aunt Marise while I went to Victoria
University, but after a year I dropped out and came up
to Auckland.'

'Why?'

'I thought it might be easier to get a job here.'

'No—why did you drop out?'

'A number of reasons.' Absently, Felicia reached out
to a bunch of firm, oval green grapes and twisted one
off. 'I didn't see much point in any of it, although the
study was enjoyable enough.'

'What else?'

'I felt rather in the way, living with Marise. She'd never
wanted children herself, and it was a bit thick being
saddled with her sister's offspring. And yet she wouldn't
hear of me going to a hostel, or flatting.'

'She never married?'

'No.' Felicia glanced at him, absently rolling the grape in her fingers. 'No, but she had a long-term lover, a politician. *He* was married. That was another problem, having me in the house. It made him very nervous. They used to pretend he was just a friend, but that became a bit difficult to sustain.'

'You must have missed ... your family. Your parents.'

Her throat suddenly constricted, Felicia nodded, and for something to do, some excuse not to have to say anything, she popped the grape into her mouth and bit into it. It was seedless, sweet with an underlying tartness.

Joshua said, 'You were the only child? Except for ... I mean, of your mother?'

'Yes.' She didn't even remember her father, who had left before she was three years old and gone to Australia. There was some talk of contacting him after her mother died, but no one could trace him. Felicia had been seven when her mother met and married Genevieve's father, an easygoing, soft-faced man who had taken Felicia to his heart.

Despite the gap in age between them and the fact that Genevieve was living away from home while she pursued an uneven career in modelling, Felicia's new stepsister had quickly earned her adoration. Dropping in for occasional visits, she brought exciting gifts for Felicia and her mother—often samples that she had been given by the manufacturers after working on an advertisement.

After Felicia entered her pre-pubescent growth spurt Genevieve encouraged her to straighten her shoulders and stop trying to disguise her true height, telling her she had the potential for modelling.

When Felicia laughed Genevieve said, 'No, I mean it. In a few years when you've grown boobs—and you don't want them too big—with those legs and those eyes you'll wow them on the catwalk, honestly. Of course, you'll have to get your teeth straightened, but that's no problem.'

Genevieve had not lived to see that happen, and by the time Felicia had developed her modest bosom she had no real ambition to be a model, but she was still grateful for the boost to her self-confidence that her stepsister's interest had brought about.

'So you ran away to Auckland?' Joshua asked, reminding her what they'd been talking about.

'I didn't run away. I left.'

'What did your aunt have to say about that?'

'Not a lot. She must have been relieved. I suppose she felt honour-bound to do her duty by me, and if I'd moved out to live in the same city it would have been like saying she'd failed to provide me with a proper home. Aunt Marise hates to do anything less than perfectly.'

'She doesn't seem to have been exactly perfect as a surrogate parent.'

'She did her best. It isn't her fault that she got lumbered with the job. Even if she'd tried, nobody could have taken my mother's place.'

Joshua nodded. 'I've been lucky; my mother and father are still alive and well, and I can't imagine calling anyone else Mum or Dad.'

'My stepfather was very good to me,' she said. 'I called him Pop.' She began fiddling with the grapes again, pulling another off the stem. She had told Joshua too much, she thought. She didn't want him prying into her life, and she didn't need to know any more about his than she knew already. She would *not* start returning his questions.

Joshua took a slice of Tararua off the small wedge on the board. He seemed intent on sampling every one of the cheeses. Felicia ate another grape.

In China he had mentioned that he was one of a family of five, coming right between two older brothers and two younger sisters. Beyond the information that she'd been an only child she had avoided talking about her own family.

'I can't imagine being an only child, either,' Joshua said, as if tuning in to her thoughts. 'My brothers and sisters are pretty important to me.'

'Genevieve was important to me,' she said. 'We might not really have been sisters, but she was the nearest I had.'

He was cutting into a miniature round of Gouda. She saw the curved knife stop midway, pause infinitesimally before he pushed it down to the wood and the yellow wedge of cheese fell away. He transferred it to his plate, reaching for another cracker. 'Yes,' he said. 'I do realise that.'

He glanced up, his face bland but his eyes sharply searching. 'Did you really know her very well? How much did you see of her before that summer?'

'Enough.' Felicia's eyes met his with hostility. 'Her father had been married to my mother for six years. From the first she treated me like a little sister. I was a flower-girl at her wedding.' Dressed in imported sky-blue silk, with a coronet of flowers on her hair, she'd been so proud of the honour of leading the procession down the aisle—four adult bridesmaids, followed by Genevieve looking breathtaking in a wonderful bridal gown from one of

Europe's top design houses, paid for by her new husband.

'She was married young,' Joshua said. The piece of cheese lay forgotten on his plate. He still held the cracker.

'Just twenty-one.'

He glanced at her in apparent surprise. 'I thought she was even younger.'

'Where did you get that idea?'

Joshua placed the cracker at last on his plate. 'From her,' he said.

'You must have misunderstood.'

There was a tiny silence. 'Paul was certainly considerably older, wasn't he?'

'He took advantage of her.'

Joshua's brows shot up. '*He* took advantage—?'

Felicia's eyes flashed warningly. 'We weren't going to discuss this.'

'We wouldn't be if you hadn't started it,' he reminded her. 'How did Paul take advantage of her?'

Unwillingly she answered, remembering snatches of the confidences Genevieve had entrusted her with through that long-ago summer. 'He...he dazzled her with his wealth, pursued her with presents and introduced her to interesting, important people, took her to fabulous places. She was young enough to be impressed by all that. We weren't poor, but my stepfather was in middle-management and my mother worked behind a shop counter for most of her life. Genevieve hadn't been accustomed to living among people with money to throw around, until she met Paul when she was on a modelling assignment.'

'So it went to her head, you think?'

'In a way. When she married Paul she thought she loved him, but she was too innocent then to realise that what she felt really was gratitude for his...apparent generosity.'

'Apparent.'

'Yes. As soon as they were married he wanted her to stop modelling and stay at home, waiting for him to have time for her—like a Barbie doll that he could pick up and play with when he felt like it.'

'It was a pretty adequate sort of home,' Joshua commented mildly.

'Oh, it was beautiful!' she agreed with faint scorn. 'Paul told her when they built it she could have anything she wanted.'

And Genevieve had. Half a dozen bedrooms, each with its own bathroom, the one she had shared with Paul when he was home furnished with a romantic opulence that had reminded the impressionably young Felicia of fairy-tale illustrations, as had Genevieve's private sitting room. A formal dining room and two big lounges, one with a television set tucked into a corner, the other spaciously designed for entertaining the business contacts Paul brought home, and their neighbours in the exclusive seaside development where successful professionals and affluent business people and retirees had built palatial homes.

'But she was lonely,' Felicia maintained. 'Paul was obsessed with his business. Even when he was home he had no time for Genevieve. She was his trophy wife, and once he "owned" her, Genevieve's happiness wasn't important any more.' He'd had a large study where he spent many evenings working on his computer or using the telephone and fax machine to communicate with business contacts all over the world. And sometimes he was away for days at a time.

'She felt neglected?' Joshua asked. He nodded rather sardonically as if answering himself. 'And she got... bored.'

Felicia's mouth tightened. She knew what he was implying—that Genevieve had been looking round for a diversion from her role of the spoiled wife of a rich older man. And had lighted on the handsome young handyman who was paid to mow the neighbourhood lawns and clip the shrubs and hedges, including those surrounding Genevieve's dream home.

Her hand clenched on the tablecloth. 'Are you going to eat that cheese?' she asked. 'Or can we go now?'

'We can if you like, but the waiter's just bringing our coffee.'

She'd forgotten he'd ordered two cappuccinos to be served after the cheese. Joshua sat back as the waiter brought a tray to the table and put in front of them two cups and a bowl of sugar crystals and two dinner mints.

While Joshua asked for the bill and dealt with it, Felicia occupied herself spooning sugar into her cup and watching it slowly sink through the creamy foam.

The waiter departed and Joshua picked up his cup. When he replaced it in the saucer it was half-empty.

'So how did you get into the retail business?' he asked.

Relieved at the change of subject, she answered, 'I got a job in the textiles department of a big store. It wasn't exactly my first choice, but I was lucky to find work at all. One year of studying mostly history and art didn't exactly qualify me for much. I figured I should get some sort of tertiary education if I wasn't going to spend the rest of my life as a shop assistant. So I enrolled in night classes.'

'Not history and art, I take it?'

She shook her head. 'At first I took a course in textiles so I'd know more about what I was doing all day. Then I considered moving into another field altogether, and spent a year learning about computers and word processing and accounting programs. Business studies seemed the way to independence, so the following year I enrolled for that—and met Shelley.'

'Your partner. She seems a pretty clued-up lady.'

'She is. She'd been managing a lunch bar in the central business district, but wanted to strike out on her own in a small enterprise that wasn't food-based. Her husband is an accountant, and after we finished our course he helped us to set up the shop. He still checks our accounts for us every year.'

'You would have needed capital.'

'My mother and stepfather left some money that my aunt invested for me, along with the proceeds from the sale of the house. There was enough for me to buy a half-share of the business.' She picked up her cup and sipped at the bittersweet liquid.

Joshua was frowning. 'Genevieve told me that everything her father had was left to her when he died, and that it didn't amount to much.'

'I suppose compared to what Paul had it didn't seem much.' Felicia was puzzled. Why would Genevieve have thought she was her father's sole beneficiary?

He had liked to live well, but just a year before his death he had taken a cut in pay rather than lose his job altogether when the company was restructured. Her mother had said they would have to wait to have Felicia's teeth fixed because they couldn't afford the expense. They'd let the insurance on the boat lapse before the accident, but there had been a house and a car. Felicia had vaguely supposed those assets were jointly owned, and that realising them had resulted in a healthy sum.

She assumed that on their parents' simultaneous demise the estate had been split between their two daughters. It had never occurred to her to ask the exact terms. At the time she'd been too young to consider the legal issues involved. But when a dentist had suggested her aunt consult an orthodontist about her teeth there had been no quibble about paying for the expensive treatment. Marise had told her they would use the money left to her by her parents, of which Marise was trustee.

On moving to Auckland Felicia had asked if some of her legacy could be used for travel expenses and to pay a bond and two weeks' rent on a flat. Marise presented her with a bank cheque that was more than adequate. As soon as she turned twenty a substantial sum representing the balance of the bequest had been transferred to her bank account, in time for her to invest most of it in the shop.

A year later, when the business seemed to have established itself on a sound footing, she had used the rest for a down payment on the flat. To Felicia it seemed there had been a lot of money. Her stepsister's scale of values had no doubt been different after living with Paul.

'Well,' Joshua said dryly, 'Genevieve may have been fantasising.'

Felicia's hackles rose. 'You say that as if it was a habit of hers.'

His lips compressed. 'Let's not get into that. You did mention you'd like to go?'

'Yes.' There was no point in starting another argument. She picked up her bag.

Joshua quickly came round the table and pulled back her chair.

They had to wait in the lobby while someone brought his car. Felicia stared straight ahead at the glass doors, the antagonism that had seemed muted for much of the evening beginning to return.

On the way home she met Joshua's efforts at conversation with chilly monosyllables, until he drew up outside her home and said, 'I don't suppose I can hope for a goodnight kiss.'

'In your dreams!' She was ashamed of the instant response just the thought of it evoked.

'Oh, my dreams!' he said softly. 'Now there, you do more than kiss me. *Much* more. All that we did in Guangzhou ... and there wasn't much that we didn't get around to, was there? At least I have the memory to draw on.'

'You're disgusting!' Felicia fumbled in the dark for the door handle. She could feel her skin warming, and treacherous memories rose to haunt her.

'What's disgusting about it?' He leaned over and closed his hand unerringly over the catch but didn't open it. 'You didn't think so at the time.'

'How would you know?' He was much too close, although he wasn't touching her at all. His arm was a barrier, preventing her from moving. Desperately, she threw at him, 'Couldn't you tell I was faking it?'

Joshua shook his head. 'Some things can't be faked. Oh, maybe you started off thinking you could go through with it cold-bloodedly, but it wasn't long before you forgot what it was all about and simply enjoyed yourself, was it? You can't tell me that what I felt in my arms, and with my tongue, my mouth, my hands, was *fake*, Felicia.'

'Sex,' she said, her voice shaking despite herself. 'An automatic reaction to physical stimulus. It means nothing.'

'Oh, yeah?' His face was inches from hers, his eyes brilliant even in the dim glow of the nearest streetlight. 'If I kissed you now it would have exactly the same effect—wouldn't it?'

Her lips were dry. She fought an urge to moisten them with her tongue—it would look like an invitation. 'If it did,' she said, 'it still wouldn't mean anything.'

He murmured, his voice so low it was scarcely more than a breath, 'Do you want me to?'

'No.' A lie. Damn him, her whole body was crying out for him and he knew it.

He leaned closer, and she shut her eyes involuntarily, holding her breath. Then she felt the cool air invade the car and realised that he had thrust open the door and moved back to his own seat to do the same on his side.

She stumbled out, but he was beside her before she had time to push the door to behind her. Felicia whirled and almost ran up the path, knowing he was following.

As she put her key in the lock he said, 'We must do this again.'

'I don't think so.' She threw open the door.

'Scared?'

'I'm not scared of you!' She injected as much scorn into her voice as she could.

'You've no need to be,' he responded imperturbably. 'You're scared of yourself, aren't you? Scared that you can't handle it...that if you see me any more you'll break down and beg me to make love to you again.'

'I'll see you in hell first!' Felicia stepped inside and turned, ready to slam the door in his face.

He stopped it with a hand on the edge, easily holding it against her efforts. 'I thought that was what you wanted,' he said. 'To see me in hell. Isn't it?'

'Yes!'

'Sure.' He looked down at her speculatively. 'Then if you're not afraid of succumbing to my irresistible charm, and you enjoy tormenting me, you'll come out with me again...won't you? Or,' he added as she glared impotently up at him, 'don't you dare?'

CHAPTER TEN

SHE shouldn't have let him get to her, manipulate her into accepting the implicit challenge. That she did so was, she recognised dimly, due as much to her own ambivalent feelings as to her fighting spirit.

Joshua would have to give up and go home eventually, she told herself. He had a business to run in Palmerston North; he couldn't stay forever in Auckland. Shamingly, she wanted to make the most of their time together, to store up memories for the inevitable parting. Because next time, she knew, he wouldn't be coming back.

He took her to a New Zealand-made film, to a play at the university theatre, to dinner again—always places with plenty of other people about—and one night to a party given by friends of his who lived in Auckland and were celebrating their wedding anniversary.

If she'd wanted to she could have embarrassed him thoroughly that evening with some of the barbed remarks that he habitually met with a wry smile and narrowed, gleaming eyes. But his friends didn't deserve to have their happy occasion marred by a couple sniping in public, so Felicia held her tongue and smiled a lot. And after the first hour she found herself enjoying the party. Joshua knew a number of people there, all of them delighted to see him.

'So what brings you up from the wilds of Palmerston North?' one large, rumpled man asked, grinning at him. He glanced interestedly at Felicia.

'Palmerston North is a respectable city with a university and all mod cons,' Joshua said. 'I have...business up here.'

'Not much farm machinery needed in Auckland.' His friend grinned again. 'You've done all right out of it, haven't you, mate? Believe you're a millionaire these days, eh?' Looking again at Felicia, he asked, 'Are you going to introduce me?'

'Soon as you stop talking,' Joshua offered. 'Felicia, for my sins this is my cousin, Vernon Weekes—Felicia Stevens.'

The big man enthusiastically engulfed her hand in his hot, beefy clasp. 'Pleased to meet you, Felicia. What's a nice girl like you doing with a rich, handsome bastard like him?' Vernon flung back his head and roared at his own joke.

'I might disagree with you over parts of that description,' Felicia said.

'What—bastard?' Vernon laughed again, missing Joshua's rueful shake of his head as he raised his brows at Felicia, his eyes filled with laughter.

Felicia, curbing an impulse to laugh with him, tore her gaze away as Vernon said, 'OK, I'll admit he's not such a bad bloke. I gave him his start, you know.'

Totally at sea, Felicia tried an enquiring smile.

'Yeah.' Vernon slapped Joshua's shoulder. 'That's right, isn't it, Josh?' Without waiting for a reply he went on, 'He took over my lawnmowing round for me when my parents carted all of us kids away for a holiday in Australia, my last year at school, and asked him to house-sit for the summer. By the time I came home my machines were running so sweet they could just about sing "God Defend New Zealand". And old Josh here had wangled himself the offer of a job for the next holidays. One of my customers had rented out his place for the holidays to the manager of an engineering firm in Whangarei. I tell you, this guy owes everything to me, eh, Josh?'

'Too true,' Joshua agreed cordially. 'I'm eternally grateful, Vern.'

'When Josh finished university he went to work for them full time. After a couple of years he branched out on his own,' Vernon beamed, 'and never looked back.' He lifted the glass in his hand and, finding it empty, said, 'I'm off for a refill. Can I get anything for you two?'

Felicia, with a half-glass of white wine, and Joshua both declined the offer, and Vernon wandered off.

'What were you doing before you went to university?' Felicia asked Joshua, puzzled by Vernon's revelations. How little she had really known him, the object of her girlish illusions. It hadn't occurred to her that his handyman job was only a temporary fill-in.

'Before? I was at school. As soon as I left I enrolled in the School of Engineering for a degree.'

Felicia stared. 'But...'

She distinctly recalled Genevieve confiding in her, 'It's so nice to be with someone my own age. Joshua understands me, you see. He treats me like an equal, not a stupid child.'

'You were still a student,' she said, 'when...when you worked for Paul and Genevieve?' Her thoughts were reeling as she tried to readjust.

'Just about to begin my third year at university. The offer to stay in my uncle and aunt's house was a great chance to study, and live for free through the holidays.

Taking on Vern's rounds gave me a bit of money to help me through to my finals, besides making sure he didn't lose customers. And I was able to do a few extra handyman jobs to earn more.'

As he had for Genevieve. He'd fixed the leaking outside tap without being asked, when he noticed it, and then Genevieve had offered to pay him to put a new washer into one in the bathroom. After that there had been the creaking hinge on the lounge door, the toilet that wouldn't completely stop flushing, the food processor that suddenly lost power, the high swinging light over the stairs that needed its bulb changed...

'How old are you?' Felicia asked blankly. In Beijing she'd thought that he looked younger than his age. It had almost counted as another strike against him.

'I'm thirty-two.' Joshua slanted another glance at her, his mouth turning up at the corners. 'You didn't know?'

'I thought...I thought you were about thirty-seven.'

'I'm shattered.'

Rapidly doing the arithmetic, she came up with the startling answer. 'Then...that summer, you were—?'

'Coming up to twenty,' he answered, looking at her curiously. 'It never occurred to me that you didn't know.'

'No,' she said. 'I had no idea.'

She had taken Genevieve far too literally. Married to a man eighteen years older than herself, Genevieve would naturally think of someone five or even six years younger as being in her own age group.

Felicia remembered exactly how Joshua had looked back then. Not a gangly teenager with smooth or fuzz-downed cheeks like the older boys at her school, but a full-grown man with broad, muscled shoulders and a dark shadowy stubble if he hadn't shaved that day. A man who had stirred barely understood but almost shamefully exciting feelings in her.

She had peeked at him from behind curtained windows and screening bushes, and once spent at least twenty minutes hidden among wind-shivered spinifex on the low sandhills above the beach, watching him do nothing but lie face down on his towel while his lean, tanned, glistening body dried after a swim. But they had seldom spoken. She was too shy and tongue-tied to initiate a conversation, and he had scarcely noticed her existence.

'I thought you were Genevieve's age.' He hadn't been exaggerating when he'd characterised his younger self as 'callow'. At nineteen it was entirely possible.

'And I thought Genevieve was twenty-one.'

Their hostess breezed up to them. 'Joshua—how are you? I've hardly had a chance to talk to you and...Felicity, is it?'

Joshua corrected her and she said, 'Sorry, Felicia. I'm so glad you came. Are you two...' her eyes darted to Joshua's face and back to Felicia's '...together?'

Felicia shook her head quickly, and Joshua said, 'Cilla, when are you going to learn discretion?'

Cilla's brown eyes danced with devilment. 'What's that? Not a way to find out anything, that's for sure. Go on, get me another lime and tonic while I have a heart-to-heart with your girlfriend, here.'

'The first thing she'll tell you is she isn't my girlfriend.' Not being given much choice, Joshua took the glass Cilla thrust at him. Turning to Felicia, he added, 'Will you feel safe if I leave you with this female barracuda for a minute?'

'You can refill my glass too,' she told him, downing the remaining wine. '*I* feel perfectly safe.' She flashed him a brilliant, false smile as she uttered the veiled threat.

His answering smile shook her to her toes. Most times he met her covert goading with a stubborn imperviousness, the only signs of anger the rigidity of his features and a warning glitter in his eyes that made her blood run hot and heavy, and her head sing with a strange elation because she knew she'd got under his skin. He might give a tight, leashed grin that acknowledged a hit but hinted at the sure knowledge that it was his considered choice not to retaliate. And that she was playing a dangerous game in trusting to his self-control.

But this smile was different. It was slow and tender, and his eyes held not anger hidden by an act of will, but warmth with a tinge of sadness, and something that could only be affection. And it took the breath right out of her body.

Cilla had noticed too. As Joshua turned away with their glasses she said softly, 'Wow! You lucky girl.'

Felicia, her lips parted in astonishment, had been following Joshua's progress across the room to the makeshift bar in the kitchen. With an effort she turned an enquiring gaze to her hostess.

Cilla grinned, regarding her with frank speculation. 'I've never seen Joshua look at a girl quite like that. Not,' she added thoughtfully, 'that I've seen him with many girls. A bit of a loner, our Josh.'

'A loner?'

'Oh, he's got lots of friends, some of them women, but he's always seemed too busy for a serious relationship. He built his own business up from scratch, you know. With a bit of help from his family in the early

days—loans and that. Well, I suppose you do know.
You're obviously close—why did he say you're not his
girlfriend?'

'We . . . we're not that close,' Felicia said. 'We knew
each other years ago, but not well. We've only been going
out together for a few weeks.'

'Really?' Cilla swivelled to stare in his direction, but
he'd disappeared into the kitchen. 'He must have fallen
like a ton of bricks. I hope it's mutual. We're awfully
fond of Joshua. It's about time he got himself hitched
and settled down to raise a family.'

Felicia gave a protesting, half-hysterical little laugh.
'Joshua, settle down?'

'He's ready for it.' Cilla regarded her shrewdly. 'But
maybe you're not. What do you do for a crust, Felicia?'

Glad of the change of subject, Felicia was still
answering questions about her work when Joshua returned with their refills.

The rest of the evening passed in a blur. Joshua never
left Felicia's side again, and she was continually conscious of him—his deep voice as he conversed easily with
the other guests, the light touch of his hand when he
guided her to a seat, his sleeve brushing her hair when
he perched himself on the arm of the big overstuffed
chair and steadied himself with a hand on the back of
it.

On the way home well after midnight he asked, 'Did
you have fun regaling Cilla with your assessment of my
character and an account of my various sins?'

'I wouldn't do that.'

'I thought you'd relish the chance.'

Suddenly depressed, Felicia shook her head and gazed
out at the passing streetlights, the sparse night-time sub-

urban traffic. He glanced at her, his head briefly turning, and returned his attention to the road.

Drawing up outside her flat, he said, 'You didn't enjoy yourself tonight?'

'It was a lovely party,' she said honestly. Cilla and her husband radiated happiness after five years of marriage, and near the end of the evening had announced that their first child was on the way and that they were thrilled to share the news with their friends. Their uninhibited delight had spilled over to the guests, and it wasn't their fault that Felicia had felt out-of-focus, an outsider looking wistfully on at other people's joyous celebration.

'I can't go on with this,' she said, speaking her thoughts aloud.

What right did she have to judge another person? She had accused Joshua of arrogance, but hadn't she displayed the same quality, taking it upon herself to punish him? His friends saw him as a good person, someone who deserved the best in life. If he'd made a mistake years ago, if even now he couldn't see that his actions had led to his lover's death, it wasn't up to her to make him face it. Whatever he had done or not done was between him and his conscience. She'd made him a scapegoat for her own sense of guilt, her failure to provide enough love and support for her beloved stepsister to stave off the despair that had led to Genevieve's last, desperate act of self-annihilation.

'What do you mean?' Joshua's voice was hushed.

'I can't... see you again.'

'*Can't?*' There was a harshness now, as if his throat felt raw.

'I won't,' Felicia said stubbornly, forcing the words out. 'This is the end, Joshua. I can't take any more.'

She felt tears threaten stingingly and made to get out of the car, but he grabbed at her hand, holding it so tightly she thought the bones might crack. He loosened his grip almost immediately, but there was no way she could have escaped it. 'Lissa!' he said.

Clamping her teeth together to stop the tears from falling, she said, *'Let me go!'*

He dropped her hand as though it had burned. His other hand clenched hard on the rim of the steering wheel. 'I'm sorry,' he said.

'I'm sorry too,' she managed to whisper, wrenching open the door at last. 'Please don't come in. Just...leave me alone.'

She had reached the sanctuary of her flat and closed the door behind her, leaning weakly against the wood, before she heard him start the engine and drive away.

Her aunt Marise came up from Wellington for a conference, and although she declined Felicia's invitation to stay in the flat, they lunched together before Marise returned to the capital.

As they waited for their salads to arrive Felicia reflected that Marise was much more at ease with her now than she had ever been when they lived in the same home. Although Marise had tried hard to replace the mother Felicia had lost, and given up a great deal of her precious privacy to raise her niece, the older woman related to adults far better than children. She'd asked Felicia to drop the title of 'Aunt' when she reached eighteen, and was content to treat her as an equal.

While they ate, Marise gave her a brief résumé of the conference and asked how business was.

'Fine,' Felicia told her. 'We're moving stock so fast it's hard sometimes to keep up.'

'And China? That must have been interesting.'

Felicia's throat momentarily closed before she managed to give a skimmed-over account of her holiday.

They were on to coffee before she said quietly, 'Marise, how much money did my mother and stepfather leave me?'

Marise finished stirring her coffee and put down her spoon. 'I don't remember exactly.'

'That,' Felicia said gently, 'is a thumping lie, isn't it? In money matters you always know precisely what's what.'

Marise bridled. 'I won't have you calling me—'

'I'm sorry,' Felicia said. 'But I can't believe you don't know how much you've spent on me. And it was your money, wasn't it? Not my mother's—she had very little— or Pop's. Genevieve was his daughter, and he never legally adopted me, although he was good to me. Whatever he had went to her, didn't it?'

Marise said, looking slightly harassed, 'He didn't apparently make a will at all, and as your mother died with him . . .'

'So you picked up the tab for me and told me I had a legacy.' Impulsively, she reached out her hand and covered her aunt's. 'Thank you. You've been much more generous than I ever knew.'

Marise flushed, and fidgeted in her chair. 'No,' she said. 'I can't accept your gratitude for something I haven't done, Felicia.'

'You...didn't?' So sure she had worked it out, Felicia was stunned.

'Not that I would have grudged...and I was more than able to keep you, but I couldn't have afforded so much...'

'But if you didn't provide the money where on earth did it come from?' She had no other relative in the world.

'I can't tell you. I promised.'

'When I was a child,' Felicia said, staring at her. 'Don't you think I have a right to know now? I owe it to whoever it was to at least thank them!'

'I've always thought you should be told,' Marise admitted. 'Especially since you seemed so set against him. It really wasn't fair when he was being so very kind to you. It isn't as though he was obliged...'

'*Who?*' Felicia demanded almost fiercely. 'You can't not tell me now. Heavens, I can probably find out anyway. There must be records of some sort.'

Marise gave up the obvious inward struggle. 'It was Paul,' she said at last. 'Genevieve's husband.'

'Why?' Felicia regarded the silver-haired man she had tracked down to his luxurious penthouse apartment on Auckland's North Shore.

Paul had scarcely changed except for the completion of the greying process. He had always been very self-contained with a courteous but aloof manner that had intimidated her as a child, and had made Genevieve weep at his coldness.

'Please sit down.' Paul indicated one of two milky cream leather sofas and waited for her reluctant compliance. 'May I offer you a drink, Lissa? Now you're all grown up.'

'Thank you, no. I don't want a drink, I want answers.'

Paul smiled, shrugged and sat down opposite her, his arm lying along the back of the sofa. Rather austerely he said, 'I trusted your aunt to keep a secret.'

'I more or less forced her to tell me. I thought it was her, you see, and she didn't feel she should take the credit for your generosity.'

'Was she good to you, Lissa?'

The question threw her. His tone sounded as if he genuinely cared. Startled, she looked into his eyes and saw there concern and compassion. 'Yes,' she said slowly, trying to come to terms with this new view of him. 'She was good to me. She loved my mother, and for her sake she made room in her life for me. It wasn't easy, and she must have sacrificed a good deal. She provided a sense of security that I badly needed, even loved me in her way. We're good friends. But you . . . I'm nothing to you! Why did you give me all that money?'

'I have plenty of that,' Paul said gently, looking around them. She didn't need to follow his gaze to assess the value of the furniture, the original paintings on the walls, the bronze sculpture standing before the big window that afforded a magnificent view of the harbour. The apartment itself must be one of the most desirable pieces of real estate in the city. 'And Genevieve was fond of you. I suppose I did it for her. In memory of her.'

Felicia swallowed around a sudden lump in her throat. 'You . . . you did love her after all,' she said huskily, making a discovery.

'Everyone loved Genevieve,' Paul said. 'She was very . . . lovable.'

The dry note in his voice made her shift uneasily. 'She thought . . .'

'I know,' Paul said when she hesitated. 'Genevieve thought I didn't care for her any more. She was wrong. I just...couldn't bear the knowledge that she was...unsatisfied.' As Felicia stiffened, her eyes widening, a flash of humour lit his face. 'Oh, I don't mean what you're thinking. No doubt in your young eyes I rated as a real Methuselah. Perhaps in Genevieve's eyes too. But I was perfectly able to make love to my wife—and make it enjoyable for her. She had no complaints in that direction.'

'Then why...?'

'Why was she not content with me?' Paul shrugged. 'A craving for excitement, or some deep need to affirm her own youth and beauty. She was terrified of losing her looks. Sometimes I think her early death was a blessing, that she'd have preferred it to growing old and finding her first wrinkle, her first grey hair. Possibly that's why she invited it.' His eyes had darkened and were looking beyond Felicia, or perhaps inward, to some poignant, haunting memory. 'Maybe,' he said almost to himself, 'it wasn't the baby at all.'

'Baby?' Felicia repeated stupidly. *'Baby?'*

Paul snapped himself to full consciousness. 'I'm sorry, I'd forgotten you wouldn't know. Of course we kept it from you at the time.' He paused. 'Genevieve was nine or ten weeks pregnant when she died.'

The news hit her like a wall. For long seconds she couldn't speak. Then his previous remarks began to penetrate her shocked brain. 'You think she killed herself because of it? But...that makes no sense!' Genevieve had never expressed any desire for a family, but surely there was no need to take her own life to avoid bearing a child?

Paul said, 'Of course it doesn't make sense.' He got up and walked away, turning his back to her while he stared out of the window, one hand dug into his pocket, the other hanging at his side. Felicia watched as it clenched and unclenched, restlessly.

Her voice hushed and hopeless, her hands growing cold, she said, 'It must have been a blow . . . losing your child as well as your wife.'

'It wasn't mine.' Paul swung to face her. 'I'm sterile. I warned Genevieve before she married me that I couldn't give her children. She was adamant that she never wanted any. The physical changes of pregnancy were repugnant to her, and she was afraid of pain.'

Felicia felt momentarily dizzy, the breath leaving her lungs.

Paul stared at the floor for a long moment, then looked up, his lips twisting. 'The ironic thing is, I would probably have accepted her child as my own once the first . . . disappointment was over. It wasn't as though I didn't know about her . . . outside activities. She never troubled herself much to conceal them from me.'

He didn't even sound particularly bitter, just sad and hurt and trying very hard and almost successfully to hide it, with his quiet, disciplined voice and his casual stance.

Was it possible that his apparent coldness, the distance he had kept between himself and his wife that summer, had been an attempt to minimise the damage to a wounded heart? 'You still loved her,' Felicia said, her own heart leaden and aching.

'To the end,' he agreed. 'Oh, not as I had when I fell head over heels like a boy in the throes of his first affair and foolishly asked her to marry me. And not the way mature people love each other, as equals. More as one might love a wayward child who is too young to know that certain things are breakable and can never be repaired. Genevieve was a lovely young thing who had never really grown up. Even you, Lissa, at only thirteen, were more mature than she would ever have been.'

But not mature enough to comprehend the undercurrents that had swirled about her, to recognise that her beloved stepsister was less perfect, less wronged than she would have had Felicia believe.

'Oh, Paul—I'm so sorry,' she said. 'I never realised...'

Carrying messages from Genevieve to Joshua had been little more than a game. Buoyed by a sense of importance that her stepsister considered her old enough to be trusted with grown-up secrets, she had accepted blindly all Genevieve's criticisms of her husband, and sympathised with her starry-eyed infatuation with a new, younger, more exciting man. Only now, with the aid of Paul's clear yet bittersweet vision, did she recognise the truth of Genevieve's essential, immutable immaturity, and how inappropriate it had been for Genevieve to make a confidante of her and employ her as a go-between.

Paul accepted her expression of regret with a sad smile. 'I know you worshipped her.'

'If I'd been older—wiser...'

'My dear child, you were far too young to influence her. You mustn't blame yourself for what happened to your sister. Do you know what I think?' Paul said. 'I don't think she really expected to die. She turned the wheel on a sudden whim, in a moment of despair, but she thought she would miraculously survive and that we would all be so happy that we would forgive her anything... and make everything come out right for her.' He shook his head. 'My poor, sweet, self-deluding Genevieve.'

CHAPTER ELEVEN

JOSHUA was sitting at his office desk in Palmerston North
when his secretary opened the door and said, 'There's
someone here to see you.'

He looked up, and Felicia slipped past the woman and
walked towards him, planting herself before the desk.

Joshua put down the pen in his hand and slowly stood
up. 'All right, Dorothy.' Looking past Felicia to his secretary, he added, 'Hold any calls that come through,
will you? Tell them I'll ring back.' He waited until the
woman had closed the door, then indicated a chair to
Felicia and said, 'So what brings you here?'

She sat down, holding her back straight so that it didn't
touch the chair. 'I want to ask you something.'

Joshua resumed his own seat, gently moving the swivel
chair from side to side, elbows supported on its leather-
covered arms, his hands loosely clasped together before
him as he looked at her with guarded eyes.

He must have been overworking, Felicia thought. He
looked thinner—his cheekbones more prominent, the
skin beneath them taut and hollowed. 'What?' he
prompted her as she continued to stare at him.

'Why didn't you phone me at home when you found
out where I lived? Why did you come to the shop
instead?'

The only hint of his surprise was the sudden cessation

of movement. 'You came all the way from Auckland to ask me that?'

She'd flown down as soon as she could without leaving Shelley unfairly in the lurch. It was Friday afternoon, and she had promised to return by Monday. 'I have some other questions as well.' But this one had been nagging at her on and off. Seemingly unimportant, it had assumed perhaps unnatural proportions in her mind.

He said, 'It would have been an invasion of your privacy, and might even have been frightening. You hadn't given your home address to Suzette, and I didn't like the idea of harassing you.'

'Even though you were angry with me? And you thought—*knew*—I had used you and thrown you over, deliberately put you down in front of a whole crowd of people?'

'Crazy, isn't it? I told you it was complicated.'

'Complicated?' Felicia shook her head. It was so simple she couldn't understand now why the glaring truth hadn't struck her weeks ago. Even when he was justifiably furious Joshua had held back from intimidating or terrorising her, from anything that would have made her truly fear him. 'It's very clear. Thank you.'

He looked at her quizzically. 'You said you have other questions.'

'Yes.' Felicia quelled a flutter of nerves in her stomach. 'I'd rather go somewhere more private, if that's possible. How...how much longer do you have to be here? Will you mind if I wait for you?'

He considered for a seemingly endless moment. 'I'm the boss,' he said finally. 'We can go now. My place?'

He was looking at her with a hard, enquiring stare as if he expected her to object, but instead she nodded and stood up.

Joshua did the same, without taking his eyes off her, and snatched up the jacket hanging on the back of his chair. 'Let's go, then.'

He ushered her out and said to his secretary, 'I'm taking the rest of the day off. Hold the fort, will you?'

The woman nodded, trying not very successfully to conceal her curiosity. 'The lady's bag?' she said tentatively.

'Bag?' Joshua looked at Felicia. She had a soft leather bag over the shoulder of the oatmeal linen jacket she wore with matching easy-fit trousers and a red blouse.

'Thank you.' She smiled at the secretary and stepped forward to pick up the small overnighter that she'd left by the desk.

She had nearly reached the outer door before Joshua moved forward and almost snatched the bag from her hand, saying roughly, 'I'll take that.'

He lived in a spacious single-storey architect-designed house set in tree-shrouded grounds on the outskirts of the city. They went from the internal garage where Joshua had parked into an L-shaped passageway. Felicia glimpsed a kitchen on one side and utility room on the other before he ushered her around the corner and through a door into a big, airy room furnished with wide linen-covered chairs that invited lounging, and featuring a fireplace screened with a brass curtain.

'Make yourself comfortable,' he said. 'I want to freshen up and get rid of this suit and tie.' He paused in the doorway. 'There's a washroom just inside the door where we came in if you need it.'

She went to explore and found a gleaming green-tiled room with a shower, toilet and wash basin. Before leaving it she took a travelling toothbrush and a miniature toothpaste tube from her shoulder bag and used them vigorously, wishing she had skipped the meal offered during the flight from Auckland. Her stomach felt decidedly uncomfortable.

There was no sign of Joshua as she made to return, but the sound of a shower running abruptly stopped as she came to a door standing ajar almost opposite the lounge. She paused, seeing the corner of a bed covered with a silver-grey quilted throwover.

She pushed at the door. The room was empty, but muted sounds came from behind another door set between two built-in wardrobes. It was a large room and against one wall was a dressing table in some light wood, while under a big window stood a wide couch upholstered to match the bedcover. On the bed Joshua had carelessly thrown down a pair of cotton slacks, some dark green briefs, and a striped green and black shirt.

The door to the *en suite* bathroom was flung open and Joshua emerged. A large towel effectively screened his naked torso while he rubbed at his hair, his head bent.

He raised it as he strode towards the bed, then stopped short, the towel in his hands.

The stark shock in his amber eyes turned to something smouldering and dangerous as Felicia stood looking calmly back at him. 'What do you want?' he said finally.

Damp curls lay on his forehead. His shoulders were smooth and powerful, and his fingers were clenched hard in the folds of the towel.

She looked into a face that was dark and stony, and swallowed painfully, her temples pounding with tension. Keeping her voice low but determinedly steady, she said, 'I want you to make love to me.'

Long moments passed with agonising slowness. The only sound in the room was laboured breathing. She saw the pinching of his nostrils as he forced air through them. His neck was rigid, the sinews prominent, and his mouth was clamped tight.

'*No!*' He threw the towel aside as though he needed to do something violent and, leaving it crumpled on the floor, strode to the bed, uncaring of his nakedness. As she watched with dilated eyes and a peculiar pain in her chest he grabbed at the briefs, then the slacks and pulled them on, zipping up the trousers with a savage tug. He shrugged into the shirt but didn't bother to button it before turning to her even while he impatiently fastened the belt that hung in the loops of the slacks.

'No?' Felicia queried, her mouth curving in an uncertain attempt at a smile.

'Why, Lissa? So you can love me and leave me again? Twist the knife further in, exact some more vengeance for your stepsister? I have a confession to make. When I said I'd be your whipping boy it wasn't because I have a taste for penance. I hoped that eventually you'd come to see that whatever I might have been guilty of at nineteen, I've learned a lot about life since then. About love.'

'What *were* you guilty of?' she asked him.

'I thought you knew all about it,' he said caustically. 'You seemed to have it pretty well sorted out. I'm sorry to be a spoilsport, but I'm not playing this game any more.'

'Was it a game when you persuaded me to see you in Auckland, to go out with you?'

'No,' he said shortly. 'It was a mistake.'

That shook her confidence, made her fall into silence. Joshua swung away, pulled a curtain over the window and then jerked it back again. He turned, thrusting his hands into his pockets.

'Why was it a mistake?' she asked.

'You know bloody well why. Because in the end you tired of making me pay and sent me away. It wasn't what I'd...planned. If you're here because you've decided I still haven't suffered enough, you're dead wrong.' He bit off the words there as if he'd regretted them.

'I came here,' she said steadily, 'because I love you.'

His reaction was hardly what she expected. He closed his eyes and drew in a harsh breath as though she'd run a stiletto into his gut.

Felicia took a step towards him, her hand out-stretched, and he opened his eyes and said, 'For God's sake, *don't*!'

Bewildered, suddenly frightened, she whispered, 'You don't want me?'

She couldn't blame him. After what she'd done to him, put him through, no wonder she had killed his love for her. 'I'm...I'm s-sorry. I took too much for granted.'

His voice grated. 'Maybe you did.'

Felicia blinked rapidly, feeling as if her heart was turning to cold, hard stone.

'It would never work,' he said, the words seemingly torn from him. 'You'd always look on me as the man who caused your sister's death. It would sour you, make you feel guilty about being with me, about loving me. And you'd start to snipe at me, chip away at our relationship, poison it with your guilt, punishing both of us until there was nothing left. I don't want that, Felicia. I'd rather remember you as the gallant, wrong-headed, loyal person who loved me even though she couldn't forgive me.'

Her instinct was to rush into denials, explanations, tell him he was wrong, that she knew better now.

She had thought that coming to him without asking for anything from him, without insisting on hearing his version of past events, would prove her trust in him. But they had to clear the air, get everything into the open, or he would forever be waiting for her to stop trusting him again.

'All right,' she said levelly, her voice hushed. 'If you won't make love to me, why don't you tell me what really happened between you and Genevieve?'

The flare that briefly appeared in his eyes might have been hope, but it quickly died. 'No,' he said. 'It wouldn't do any good.' Taking his hands from his pockets, he came towards her. 'Where are you staying? I'll take you there.'

But Felicia stood her ground. 'I planned to stay here with you. Why wouldn't it do any good?' she demanded.

'Here? You can't.'

Brushing that aside, she repeated, 'Why wouldn't it do any good? You think I won't believe you?'

'That's certainly on the cards,' he said sardonically.

She hadn't before. But that wasn't his only reason. Looking at him, she knew what was really holding him back and said softly, 'You're afraid of hurting me, aren't you? That's why you didn't just make me listen to you, force me to accept the truth about her. You didn't want to tarnish my memories of Genevieve.'

He gazed at her in silence, and she guessed at the hope warring with his determination not to shatter her illusions. 'You've lost enough,' he said at last. 'I couldn't take that away from you too.'

Felicia shook her head. 'And the alternative is to take away the only man I'll ever love?'

His shoulders heaved. His voice thick, he choked, 'Oh, *God,* Lissa! Stop torturing me!'

'It's *all right,*' she said, and held out her arms.

He let out a great sigh, and his arms came tightly around her, his lips on her hair, her temple, her cheek, as she told him, 'I went to see Paul. Genevieve was lovely and I'll always cherish her memory, but she wasn't a saint—or an angel. She hurt people without ever meaning to. Like I hurt you. When I sent you away I was so confused. She'd said you were her age so I'd always thought you were twenty-five when...when it happened. But you were hardly more than a boy. And Joshua—darling—if you hold me any tighter I'll suffocate.'

He groaned and then laughed, and loosened his hold. 'I'm sorry. Say that again.'

'Darling? Joshua, darling, can I please stay?'

'As long as you like. Darling. Do you really want to know about Genevieve and me?'

'Not unless you want to tell me.' She looked at him with grave, clear eyes.

She felt the breath he drew in and let out again. 'Perhaps I should,' he said. 'You're entitled to know it all. Come here.'

He led her to the bed and arranged the pillows so she could sit back against them, and then with his arm about her sat by her side. 'It was brief and torrid, and half the time I was consumed by guilt and the fear of her husband finding out. The other half—I thought it was the love of a lifetime. We even talked of running away together.'

'I know,' she said, remembering Genevieve, flushed with excitement and giggling like a teenager, whispering to her as they lay on Genevieve's big bed. 'He wants me to leave Paul and be with him!' she'd said, stretching out on the satin cover, her arms above her head, eyes half-closed, her body writhing in a sensuous, catlike movement that made Felicia tingle with inexplicable embarrassment. 'Oh, it would be wonderful—to run away with Joshua and make mad, passionate love with him for the rest of my life!'

Fantasising, Felicia realised now. As if to confirm it, Joshua said, 'When I convinced her I was serious she told me I was a stupid boy and what did I think we were going to live on? I suggested we could manage on what her father had left her until I got a job and was able to support her, and she said...'

'Said what?' Felicia asked softly.

Joshua shook his head with a rueful laugh. 'It doesn't matter. At the time it stung, but then I was young and easily hurt.'

'Tell me.'

He hesitated, gave her a crooked little smile, and then capitulated. 'She said she had no intention of supporting an opportunist little gigolo on her father's money. I was stunned. And then she laughed and said surely I couldn't have thought there was anything permanent about our relationship. And in a very youthful and self-righteous way I told her I had, but she needn't expect to continue it. That was even funnier, apparently. She patted my cheek and said I was cute.'

Felicia winced. 'She told me you'd planned on going away together, but then you changed your mind and said you didn't want to be tied down.'

Joshua's smile died. 'I suppose she wanted you to keep on hero-worshipping her, so she bent the true story a bit.'

'She probably believed it by the time she told me,' Felicia guessed. 'Looking back, I can see that she used to twist things in her own mind to put herself in a good light. Paul says she never grew up.'

'In hindsight, he's probably right. I've never thought particularly about what motivated her. Once I got back to university and my extremely sane, thoroughly nutty family, I realised how lucky I was to have escaped mucking up my life completely for a bit of summer madness. I was bloody ashamed of myself and anxious to put the whole thing behind me.'

'And you didn't ever worry that her death might be connected with you?'

'I knew nothing about it for months. When Vern mentioned it in passing one day I was horrified, of course. But he said it was an accident—that she'd run into a bridge just days after Vern and his family came back from Australia and I left to re-enrol at university.'

'The coroner brought in a verdict of accident, but there was a question mark about whether he was being kind to the family, using the benefit of the doubt.'

'You thought she did it on purpose?'

'It's a perfectly straight road and a wide bridge. She was hysterical when I told her you hadn't sent any reply to her last note to you. She cried and cried, so much that it frightened me.'

Joshua frowned. 'Lissa, I *swear* she never cared that much for me. Do you know what was in the note?'

'I think so. She wanted—begged you—to take her away with you. She knew you were leaving soon, and . . . well, I thought she was so much in love with you that she just couldn't bear not to be with you.'

'If that's what was in it,' he said with scepticism, 'then she'd changed her tune drastically.' He thought for a minute. 'Paul wasn't violent, was he?'

'No, I'm sure he would never have been.' Lissa tried to think back over the years. 'She wasn't very coherent, but she said when Paul found out . . . that her marriage would be over and she'd have nowhere to go, no one to turn to. And that I should never believe anything a man told me. And . . . that the only thing left now was to end it.' Felicia took a deep, uneven breath. 'I've never told anyone about that before. I was sure the crash wasn't an accident. I was always convinced she did it because you'd turned her down.'

Joshua's voice was carefully neutral. 'Are you sure of what was in the note? She'd made it pretty plain that she wasn't interested in trading a rich, successful husband for a struggling university student. I was only good for a bit of quick, furtive sex.'

Felicia glanced up at him. 'I hadn't told her that you had torn up her note without reading it.'

'I didn't realise you were watching.'

'I hoped you might change your mind about sending a reply.'

'It was all over by then and she must have known it. You could say the scales had fallen.'

Felicia hesitated and looked down at her hands, curled together in her lap. 'Did you know...that she was pregnant?'

The silence stretched for so long that she had to look at him. His face was drawn in shock, his eyes dark and inscrutable. 'How far?'

'Nine or ten weeks, Paul said.'

Joshua let out a sighing breath. 'Then it wasn't mine,' he said. 'Thank God.'

'All that summer...?'

'No. Kisses, stuff like that, yes. But I kept trying to back off despite the temptation, and I thought she was resisting it too. All part of the game, I guess. It wasn't until after that barbecue halfway through January that we...that it happened. And only a couple more times after that.'

'But all those notes—'

'From her to me, mostly. How many times did I send notes back? Not more than twice, from memory.'

He was right, she recalled. He had taken the furtively delivered envelopes from her with scarcely a word and sent her away. And at first, according to Genevieve, the messages had been innocuous requests for him to give her lawn an extra trim before a barbecue, or lop off a tree limb damaged in a summer storm, or clean a drain.

Only later had she begun asking Felicia to slip along quietly and try not to be too obvious, hinting that the notes were lovers' missives.

'There was someone else,' Felicia said slowly.

How often had she come back from these errands or others to find that Genevieve had disappeared? She'd return an hour or so later, flushed and smiling and apologetic. 'I remembered we're clean out of bacon, and you know how annoyed Paul will be if he doesn't get his bacon and eggs on Saturday morning.' Or, 'I fancied cheesecake for dessert tonight, and just slipped out to get it. Sorry, darling, you weren't worried, were you? Of course not, you're a big girl now.'

'I know there was,' Joshua said.

Felicia turned to him in surprise.

'She threw that at me when I told her we were finished.' His mouth twisted. 'I was too young to take being laughed at.'

Felicia winced for him. 'Who?'

He shook his head. 'No idea. But she'd hoped to make him jealous by flaunting her relationship with me. I'm not sure what she expected of him, but I think he was supposed to leave his wife and "rescue" her from Paul. He must have had money.' Joshua paused. 'I'm sorry. That was unnecessary, a legacy from the past. Maybe she genuinely did care for him. Although she had her own unique way of showing it.'

'I know who it was,' Felicia realised, recalling the wealthy thirty-something futures broker who had been holidaying with his wife and family in a new two-storey mansion not far from Paul's house. Paul and Genevieve had been invited there for dinner, and the couple had attended all Genevieve's parties.

Once Felicia had come home early from the beach after being stung by a jellyfish and found the man having a drink with Genevieve on the secluded terrace at the back of the house. Felicia had put his hurried departure down to Genevieve's preoccupation with the sting as she hustled her into the kitchen to find some vinegar.

That evening Genevieve had told Paul in detail about Felicia's mishap without mentioning the futures broker—who had visited again a few days later, startling Felicia by coming out of the downstairs bathroom as she entered the house in her bathing suit and bare, sandy feet.

He had looked startled too, and muttered something about washing his hands after having had to change a tyre, lucky he'd been so handy to their place. When she stepped into the shower to wash off the sand the cubicle had been warm and steamy. Without examining the issue, Felicia had known instinctively she shouldn't mention the man's visit to Paul.

'He had children,' she said. 'And I don't think he had any intention of leaving his wife.'

'But maybe Genevieve expected him to,' Joshua suggested, 'and when he refused she turned to me, hoping I'd take her with me when I left, because she was afraid of Paul finding out about the baby?'

Felicia digested that. 'I thought she was afraid he'd find out about *you*. But you're probably right. Paul knew about her affairs, he told me. But being pregnant must have frightened her.' It wouldn't have occurred to her that Paul loved her enough to raise another man's child. She had never appreciated how much he cared for her.

'I guess…she was reacting like a child who's been caught doing something wrong—looking for any way to get out of trouble.'

Joshua said, 'Maybe that's what she meant by ending it—she was talking about ending the pregnancy.'

'But she couldn't bring herself to…or she wanted that man's child.'

'Perhaps she saw it as a bargaining counter, and when he refused to leave his family…'

Was that why Genevieve had experienced that moment of despair and turned the wheel to bring the car head-on to the concrete bridge abutment? Felicia shivered. Or…just maybe it had been an accident after all.

'Either way, she must have cared for him.'

'Possibly,' Joshua said. 'I was young then. Too young to guess at what went on in her head.'

'I never really knew her,' Felicia confessed. 'I thought she was telling me all her secrets, but she kept the most important ones from me.'

His grip tightened on her. 'Do you mind very much? I know you thought the sun rose and set on her.'

Felicia shook her head. 'It's better to mourn a real person than a mirage. I still miss her, but…now I'm all grown up I can cope with reality.'

And perhaps too, she was adult enough to forgive herself for not saving Genevieve. And for wasting so many years transferring her guilt to Joshua, blaming him because that was easier than admitting she blamed herself.

'You mean,' Joshua asked deeply, 'I haven't lost you?'

'Not unless you want to.' She twisted to face him. 'I was afraid, before, that you were telling me you didn't love me any more.'

'You don't get off that easily,' he said. 'Not easily at all.'

His lips came down on hers, fierce and seeking, and he gathered her fully into his arms.

Felicia freed an arm and flung it about his neck, unstintingly returning the kiss. 'Now will you make love to me?' she asked him when he lifted his mouth.

Joshua adjusted the pillows behind them and moved her down in the bed to lay her head on one. 'Try and stop me,' he growled.

She didn't try very hard. There didn't seem much point when he was quickly and efficiently divesting her of her jacket and her rather expensive designer pants, discarding them onto the floor with no thought for creases, along with her shoes.

He got distracted for a short time after that when she ran a hand over the bare chest that his already open shirt had revealed to her inquisitive eyes. Muttering something unintelligible, he urgently sought her mouth again, but she pushed him back against the other pillow and continued her leisurely exploration. Until he turned the tables and began to unbutton the red blouse, revealing her black lace bra and the matching panties.

He gulped in a heavy breath then, and his eyes devoured the delicate curves and concavities, almost searing her skin with the intensity of his gaze. 'I thought I'd never see you like this again,' he said. 'I thought I was dying.'

Dying? Felicia shivered. 'Don't say that,' she whispered, and with a hand behind his head brought his mouth back to hers.

She knew he wanted to make this sweet and slow, but she was starved for him, and greedy. Within minutes she was tugging at his belt, easing down the zip.

'Darling,' he protested, 'I don't know how long I can last out if you do...*oh, my God—*that!'

Felicia laughed softly and closed her teeth gently on his earlobe. 'You promised,' she said, 'if I asked...'

He had to steady his breathing. 'What exactly are you asking?' His trousers and the dark green briefs had joined her clothes on the floor beside the bed.

Felicia bit his ear a little harder, then whispered into it.

'Oh...that?' His eyes gleamed. She felt the roughness of the curled, crisp hair on his legs tickle the smooth skin of her inner thighs. 'You mean...this?'

Felicia let out a long sigh of content, her eyelids fluttering down. 'Yes,' she breathed. 'Oh...oh, yes!'

His mouth closed over hers and he began the ancient rhythm that had bonded men and women to each other since the dawn of time, the dawn of love. 'Yes?' he murmured, his mouth against her skin, and received the answering echo of her voice, and then of her body as she joined him in the moment when time and the world spun away and left them hanging in eternity with nothing but each other to cling to.

After their breathing steadied again Joshua rolled on his side and over to his back, holding her with her head resting on his shoulder. 'You are going to marry me, aren't you?' he asked. 'I hope you realise that if you ever love me and leave me again I'll follow you and drag you back by the hair, if necessary.'

'You don't mean that,' she said. 'Besides, my hair's too short.'

His chest shook in a silent laugh. 'You're right—on both counts. But I don't intend to let you go again. I'll hold you with my love, and bind you with kisses.'

'I promised Shelley I'd be back on Monday,' she told him, tracing his mouth with a fingertip. 'But after that...we'll have to make some arrangements.'

He kissed her finger, and caught her hand in his. 'We'll work it out. Somehow we've both got to be in the same city. Do you fancy a honeymoon in China?'

'Hotel guests should live in the designated rooms and beds,' she reminded him.

Joshua grinned. 'We'll ask for a double bed. We can both live in it.'

'OK,' Felicia said sleepily, rubbing her cheek against him. 'Do you want children? Your friend Cilla thinks you should settle down and raise a family.'

'Does she now? Is that why you decided to make an honest man of me?'

'You *are* an honest man,' Felicia said soberly, lifting her head to look at him. 'I'm sorry it took me so long to realise it. I think I was stuck in a time warp, desperately hanging onto my thirteen-year-old dream world. A sort of security blanket, I suppose.'

'It's understandable. What else did you have to hang onto after losing everyone you had in the world?'

'But I nearly lost you because I wouldn't let go of my childish illusions.' She ran a finger across his chest to the hollow of his throat, counting the pulse beats. 'I want children. More than one. I'd like...a girl named after Genevieve. Would you mind?'

Joshua shook his head. 'Anything you want,' he said. 'I'd like her to look like her mother. Think we can arrange that?'

'I'm sure we can,' Felicia said. 'But it will take some practice.'

'True,' Joshua agreed gravely. 'I think we should start practising right now.' And he pulled her, laughing, back into his arms.

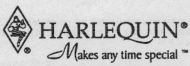

Take 2 bestselling love stories FREE

Plus get a FREE surprise gift!

Special Limited-Time Offer

Mail to Harlequin Reader Service®

3010 Walden Avenue
P.O. Box 1867
Buffalo, N.Y. 14240-1867

YES! Please send me 2 free Harlequin Presents® novels and my free surprise gift. Then send me 6 brand-new novels every month, which I will receive months before they appear in bookstores. Bill me at the low price of $3.12 each plus 25¢ delivery and applicable sales tax, if any*. That's the complete price, and a saving of over 10% off the cover prices—quite a bargain! I understand that accepting the books and gift places me under no obligation ever to buy any books. I can always return a shipment and cancel at any time. Even if I never buy another book from Harlequin, the 2 free books and the surprise gift are mine to keep forever.

106 HEN CH69

Name	(PLEASE PRINT)	
Address	Apt. No.	
City	State	Zip

This offer is limited to one order per household and not valid to present Harlequin Presents® subscribers. *Terms and prices are subject to change without notice. Sales tax applicable in N.Y.

UPRES-98   ©1990 Harlequin Enterprises Limited

DEBBIE MACOMBER

invites you to the

HEART OF TEXAS

Join Debbie Macomber as she brings you the lives
and loves of the folks in the ranching community
of Promise, Texas.

If you loved Midnight Sons—don't miss
Heart of Texas! A brand-new six-book series
from Debbie Macomber.

Available in February 1998
at your favorite retail store.

Heart of Texas by Debbie Macomber

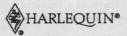

HARLEQUIN®

HPHRT1

Don't miss these Harlequin favorites by some of our bestselling authors!

HT#25721	THE ONLY MAN IN WYOMING	$3.50 U.S. ☐
	by Kristine Rolofson	$3.99 CAN. ☐
HP#11869	WICKED CAPRICE	$3.50 U.S. ☐
	by Anne Mather	$3.99 CAN. ☐
HR#03438	ACCIDENTAL WIFE	$3.25 U.S. ☐
	by Day Leclaire	$3.75 CAN. ☐
HS#70737	STRANGERS WHEN WE MEET	$3.99 U.S. ☐
	by Rebecca Winters	$4.50 CAN. ☐
HI#22405	HERO FOR HIRE	$3.75 U.S. ☐
	by Laura Kenner	$4.25 CAN. ☐
HAR#16673	ONE HOT COWBOY	$3.75 U.S. ☐
	by Cathy Gillen Thacker	$4.25 CAN. ☐
HH#28952	JADE	$4.99 U.S. ☐
	by Ruth Langan	$5.50 CAN. ☐
LL#44005	STUCK WITH YOU	$3.50 U.S. ☐
	by Vicki Lewis Thompson	$3.99 CAN. ☐

(limited quantities available on certain titles)

AMOUNT	$ _____
POSTAGE & HANDLING	$ _____
($1.00 for one book, 50¢ for each additional)	
APPLICABLE TAXES*	$ _____
TOTAL PAYABLE	$ _____
(check or money order—please do not send cash)	

To order, complete this form and send it, along with a check or money order for the total above, payable to Harlequin Books, to: **In the U.S.:** 3010 Walden Avenue, P.O. Box 9047, Buffalo, NY 14269-9047; **In Canada:** P.O. Box 613, Fort Erie, Ontario, L2A 5X3.

Name: _____

Address: _____ City: _____

State/Prov.: _____ Zip/Postal Code: _____

Account Number (if applicable): _____

*New York residents remit applicable sales taxes.
 Canadian residents remit applicable GST and provincial taxes.

Look us up on-line at: http://www.romance.net

Coming Next Month

HARLEQUIN PRESENTS®

THE BEST HAS JUST GOTTEN BETTER!

#1971 THE RELUCTANT HUSBAND Lynne Graham
Unbeknown to Frankie, her marriage to Santino had never been annulled—and now he was intending to claim the wedding night they'd never had! But Santino hadn't bargained on falling for Frankie all over again....

#1972 INHERITED: ONE NANNY Emma Darcy
(Nanny Wanted!)
When Beau Prescott heard he'd inherited a nanny with his grandfather's estate, he imagined Margaret Stowe to be a starchy spinster. But she turned out to be a beautiful young woman. Just what situation had he inherited here?

#1973 MARRIAGE ON THE REBOUND Michelle Reid
Rafe Danvers had always acted as if he despised Shaan; he even persuaded his stepbrother to jilt her on her wedding day. Yet suddenly Rafe wanted to proclaim her to the world as his wife—and Shaan wanted to know why....

#1974 TEMPORARY PARENTS Sara Wood
Laura had sworn never to see her ex-lover, Max, again. But cocooned in a cliff-top cottage with him, watching him play daddy to her small niece and nephew, it was all too easy to pretend she and Max were together again....

#1975 MAN ABOUT THE HOUSE Alison Kelly
(Man Talk!)
Brett had decided women were unreliable, and right now he wanted to be single. Or so he thought—until he agreed to house-sit for his mother, and discovered another house-sitter already in residence—the gorgeous Joanna!

#1976 TEMPTING LUCAS Catherine Spencer
Emily longed to tell Lucas about the consequences of their one-night stand eleven years ago, and that she still loved him. But she was determined that if they ever made love again, it would be he who'd come to her....